To lie with a man in a snow-filled night, safe after adversity.

A man with a man's body, a man's tastes, the smell of his skin woody and strong, his muscles even in the dimness defined and substantive. She was presented with a fine handsome man and a night that would hold no questions.

The ghost of a smile played around Bea's lips before sense reined it in. Of course she could not take advantage of the situation. She was a lady and a widow. Besides, already she thought his body had relaxed into sleep, the even cadence of his breath confirming it. To him she was nothing more than a warm skin to survive against. When the tip of her finger reached out to the ridge of his shoulderblade and traced the muscle in air, she wished that she might have been braver and truly touched him.

So unwise, another voice cautioned, the knowledge of her plainness leading only to rejection that would be embarrassing to them both.

AUTHOR NOTE

ONE UNASHAMED NIGHT is the second book in a family trilogy about the three Wellingham brothers, Asher, Taris and Cristo. Asher, the Duke of Carisbrook, appeared in HIGH SEAS TO HIGH SOCIETY, and I received many letters from fans who were fascinated by his younger brother, Taris, and wanted to read his story.

Well, here he is! Lord Taris Wellingham is an intensely private man, and one who keeps the world at bay in order to preserve his greatest secret.

Cristo's book is yet to come. He has had only a vague mention so far, but as a spy for England in France he has his own demons and distance.

I'd like to dedicate this book to three wonderful women in my life. Pat Rendall, for her insight into the world of darkness, my mother Jewell Kivell, for enthusiastically reading the first draft, and Linda Fildew, my fantastic editor, for her patience with and belief in all of my books.

ONE UNASHAMED NIGHT

Sophia James

MILLS & BOON

First published in Great Britain 2010
Harlequin Mills & Boon Limited,
Eton House, 18-24 Paradise Road, Richmond, Surrey TW9 1SR

© Sophia James 2010

ISBN: 978 0 263 21443 7

Harlequin Mills & Boon policy is to use papers that are natural,
renewable and recyclable products and made from wood grown in
sustainable forests. The logging and manufacturing process conform
to the legal environmental regulations of the country of origin.

Printed and bound in Great Britain
by CPI Antony Rowe, Chippenham, Wiltshire

Sophia James lives in Chelsea Bay, on Auckland, New Zealand's, North Shore, with her husband, who is an artist, and three children. She spends her morning teaching adults English at the local Migrant School, and writes in the afternoon. Sophia has a degree in English and History from Auckland University, and believes her love of writing was formed reading Georgette Heyer with her twin sister at her grandmother's house.

Previous novels by the same author:

FALLEN ANGEL
ASHBLANE'S LADY
HIGH SEAS TO HIGH SOCIETY
MASQUERADING MISTRESS
KNIGHT OF GRACE
MISTLETOE MAGIC
  (part of *Christmas Betrothals*)

ONE UNASHAMED NIGHT
has characters you will have met in
HIGH SEAS TO HIGH SOCIETY

Look for Cristo's story. Coming soon.

Chapter One

Maldon, England—January 1826

The darkness was pulling him down even as he fought to escape it, his eyes widening to catch a tiny tendril of light, the flare of it making him shout out, wanting it, the last colour before complete blackness enveloped him...

'Sir, sir. Wake up. It's a dream you are having.'

The voice came from somewhere close and Lord Taris Wellingham slipped from sleep and returned to the warmth of the carriage travelling south to London with a jolt. A face blurred before him, but in the dusk he could not tell whether the woman was young or old. Her voice was soft, almost musical, the lisp on the letter 's' denoting perhaps a genteel upbringing in the north?

With care he turned away, fingers stiff against the silver ball on top of his ebony cane and all his defences raised.

'I would ask for your forgiveness for my lapse in manners, madam.'

The small laugh surprised him. 'Oh. You do indeed have it, sir.'

This time there was decided humour in her tone, and something more hidden. He wished he was able to see the hue of her eyes or the shade of her hair, but any form of colour had long since gone, leached now even in full sunlight and replaced by the grey sludge of silhouette.

A netherworld. His world. And the ability to hide his disability was all the dignity left to him.

Taking a breath he held it, seeking in silence a path to follow. He pretended to read the watch on the chain at his waist, hating such deceit, but in company it was what he had been reduced to—a man on the edge of his world and in danger of falling off.

'Another hour and a half to reach our destination, I should imagine.' The woman's guess was like a gift for it gave him a timeframe, something to hang any suggestion of their whereabouts upon.

'Unless the weather worsens.' Outside he could hear a keening wind and the temperature had dropped sharply, even in the space of the moments he had been asleep. Tilting his head, he listened to the sound of the wheels beneath them and determined the snow to have deepened too.

Unexpectedly tension filled his body. Something was wrong. The whirr of the wheel on the right side was off, unbalanced, scraping against steel.

He shook away the concern and cursed his over-sensitive hearing, deeming it far better to concentrate on other things. There were four other people in the carriage, he had counted them as they got in, this woman the only one on his side. One of the gentlemen was asleep, his snores soft through the night, and the other was speaking to an older woman about household tasks and the hiring of servants. His mother, perhaps, for there was a tone in his voice suggesting affection.

The wheel was worsening, the sound underlined by a tremor in the chassis. He felt it easily in the vibration where his palm lay open against the window. No longer able to ignore danger, Taris lifted his cane and banged hard on the roof.

But it was too late! The vehicle lurched to the right as the axle snapped, the scream of the driver eerie in the darkness, the splintering of wood, the quick crunch of the door on his side against earth, the rolling shock of impact as people tumbled over and over. When his head was thrown against metal, a sharp pain followed.

And then silence.

Bodies were everywhere, the groans of the older woman taking precedence, the sobs of her son muted and fearful. The other two occupants made no noise at all and Taris's hands reached over.

The woman beside him still breathed—he could feel the warmth of air against his fingers—whilst the previously snoring gentleman had neither pulse nor breath, his neck arched at a strange angle.

Inky blackness now covered everything, the lamps gone and the moon tonight a slice of nothing.

His world! Easier than daylight. Throwing down his cane, he stood.

* * *

Beatrice-Maude Bassingstoke could barely believe what had happened. Her head ached and her top lip was cut inside.

An accident. A terrible accident. The realisation made her shake and she clamped her mouth shut to try to hide the noise as her teeth chattered together.

In the slight beam of light the dark-haired stranger gently lifted the lifeless body of a man whom she could see was well and truly dead and laid him on the floor. The older woman opposite broke into peals of panicked terror as she too registered this fact and her younger companion tried fruitlessly to console her.

'Enough, madam.' The tall man's voice brooked no argument and the woman fell silent, a greater problem now taking her attention.

'It…it is f…freezing.'

'At least we are still alive, Mama, and I am certain that this gentleman can repair things.' Her grown son looked up, supplication written on his face. He made no effort at all to rise himself, but stayed with his arm around his mother's shoulders in a vain attempt to keep her warm, for the whole side of the carriage lay buckled and twisted, the door that had been there before completely missing.

'If you will give me a moment, I will try to cover the opening.' The tall man's cape was caught by the wind as he stepped out, the crumpled chassis of the coach making his exit more difficult than it would otherwise have been. Framed by snow, she saw his hair escape the confines of his queue and fall night-black against the darkness of his clothes and she could barely wrench her eyes from his profile.

He was the most beautiful man she had ever seen! The thought hit her with all the force of surprise and she squashed down such ridiculousness.

Frankwell Bassingstoke had been a handsome man too, and look where that had got her. Swallowing, she turned back towards the woman and, rummaging in her reticule, pulled out a handkerchief and handed it over.

'Where did the man go to? Why is he not back?' The older woman's voice held panic as she took the cloth and blew her nose soundly, the hysteria of fright heightened by a realisation that their lives depended on the one who had just left them to find the missing portal. Already the temperature had dropped further; the air was harder to breath. Lord, Bea thought, what must it be like outside in the snow and the wind and the icy tracks of road with only a slither of light?

Perhaps he had perished or was in need of a voice to call him back to the coach, lost as he was in the whiteness? Perhaps they sat here as he took his last breath in a noble but futile effort to save them?

Angry both at her imagination and immobility, she wrapped her cloak around her head so that only her eyes were visible and edged herself out into the weather, meaning to help.

He stood ten yards away, easing the driver from the base of a hedge, carefully holding his neck so that it was neither jarred nor bent. He wore no gloves and the cloak he had left the carriage with was now wrapped about the injured man, a small blanket of warmth against the bitter cold. Without thick wool upon him his own shirt was transparent, a useless barrier against such icy rain.

'Can I help you?' she shouted, her voice taken by the wind and his eyes caught hers as he turned, squinting against the hail.

'Go back. You will freeze out here.' She saw the strength in him as he hoisted the driver in his arms and came towards her. Scrambling for shelter, she turned to assist him once she was back in the relative warmth of the coach.

'There is no room in here,' the old lady grumbled as she refused to shift over even a little and Beatrice swept the reticule from her own seat and crouched, her breath forming white clouds in the darkness as she replied.

'Put him here, sir. He can lie here.'

The tall man placed the other gently on the seat, though he made no effort to come in himself.

'Look after him,' he shouted and again was gone, the two other occupants silent in his wake.

One man dead, one man injured, one older woman hysterical and one younger man useless. Bea's catalogue of their situation failed to include either her injuries or that of the tall stranger, but when he had stood by the door she had noticed blood near his eye, trickling across his face and the front of his white, white shirt in a steady stream of red.

He used his hands a lot, she thought, something that was unusual in a man. He had used them to slide down the cheek of the dead gentleman opposite and across the arms and legs of the driver who lay beside her, checking the angle of bones and the absence of breath and the warmth or coldness of skin.

When she had felt his fingers on the pulse at her neck as she had awakened after the accident, warmth had instantly bloomed. She wished he might have ventured lower, the tight want in her so foreign it had made her dizzy…

Shock consumed such daydreams. She was a twenty-eight-year-old widow who had no possible need or want for any man again. Ever. Twelve years of hell had cured her of that.

The movements of the older lady and her son brought her back to the present as they tried to unwrap the driver from the cocoon of the borrowed cape and take it for their own use. Laying her hands across the material, Bea pressed down.

'I do not think that the gentleman who gave him this cloak would appreciate your taking it.'

'He is only the driver…' the man began, as if social status should dictate the order of death, but he did not continue as the one from outside appeared yet again.

'M…m…ove b…b…ack.'

His voice shook with the coldness of a good quarter of an hour out in the elements with very little on and in his hands he held the door.

Hoisting himself in, he wedged the door between the broken edges, some air still seeping through the gaping jagged holes, but infinitely better than what had been there a second earlier.

Beads of water ran down his face and his shirt was soaked to the skin, sticking against his body so that the outline of muscle and sinew was plainly evident. A body used to work and sport. Taking a cloth from her bag, Bea caught his arm and handed it to him, the gloom of the carriage picking up the white in his teeth as he smiled, their fingers touching with a shock of old knowledge.

Her world of books came closer: Chariclea and Theagenes, Daphnis and Chloe—just a few of the lovers from centuries past who had delighted her with their tales of passion.

But never for her.

The plainness of her visage would not attract a man like this one, a man who even now turned to the driver, finding his hand and measuring the beat of his heart against the count of numbers.

'You have done this before?' She was pleased her voice sounded so level-headed. So sensible.

'Many times,' he returned, swiping at hair that fell in dripping waves around his face. Long, much longer than most men kept theirs. There was arrogance in his smile, the look of a man who knew how attractive he was to women. All women. And certainly to one well past her prime.

Looking away, she hated the hammer beat of her heart. 'Will anyone come, do you think?'

Another question. This time aimed at the carriage in general.

'No one.' The younger man was quick in his reply. 'They will not come until the morning and by then Mama will be…'

'Dead…dead and frozen.' His mother finished the sentiment off, her pointless rant an extension of the son's understanding of their predicament.

'If we sit close and conserve our energy, we can wait it out for a few hours.' The stranger's voice held a strand of impatience, the first thread of anything other than the practicality that she had heard.

'And after that…?' The younger man's voice shook.

'If no one comes by midnight, I will take a horse and ride towards Brentwood.'

Bea stopped him. 'But it is at least an hour away and in this weather…' She left the rest unsaid.

'Then we must hope for travellers on the road,' he returned and brought out a silver flask from his pocket, the metal in it glinting in what little light there was.

After a good swallow he wiped the top and handed it over to her.

'For warmth,' he stated. 'Give it to the others when you have had some.' Although she was a woman who seldom touched alcohol, she did as he said, the fire-hot draught of the liquor chasing away the cold. The older woman and younger man, however, did not wish for any. Not knowing quite what to do now, she tried to hand it back to the man squeezed in beside her.

When he neither reached for it nor shook his head, she left it on her lap, the cap screwed back on with as much force as she could manage so that not a drop would be wasted. He had much on his mind, which explained his indifference, she decided, the flask and its whereabouts the least of all his worries.

Finding her own bag wedged under the seat, she brought out the Christmas cake that she had procured before leaving Brampton. Three days ago? She could barely believe it was only that long. Unfolding the paper around the delicacy, she looked up.

'Would everyone like a piece?'

The two opposite reached out and she laid a generous portion in their hands, but the tall man did nothing, merely tilting his head as though listening for something. Beatrice tried to imagine what it was that had caught his attention as she tucked the cake away. She did not take any either, reasoning perhaps he wished for her to ration the food just in case the snowstorm kept up and nobody came.

Nobody. The very word cast her mind in other directions. There would be nobody to meet her or to miss her if she failed to arrive in London. Not this week or the next one.

Perhaps the head gardener whom she had befriended in the past few weeks might one day wonder why she had never come to visit as she had promised she would, but that would be the very most of it. She could vanish here and be swallowed up by snow and her disappearance would not cause a single ripple.

Twenty-eight years old and friendless. The thought would have made her sadder if she had not cultivated her aloofness for a reason. Protection was a many-faceted thing and her solitariness had helped when Frankwell, in his last years, had become a man who wanted to know everything about everyone.

Lord, she smiled wryly. Easier than the man he had first been, at least. She felt with her forefinger for the scar that ran down from her elbow, the edges of skin healed as badly as the care she had received after the *accident* had happened. So badly, in fact, that she had worn long-sleeved gowns ever since, even in the summer.

Summer? Why was she thinking of warmth when the temperature in this coach must be way below freezing point now?

The driver groaned loudly, struggling to sit, his face a strange shade of pale as he opened his eyes.

'What happened?'

The tall man answered his question. 'The wheel fell off the carriage and we overturned.'

'And the horses? Where are the horses?'

'I tethered them under a nearby tree. They should last a few hours with the shelter the branches are affording them.'

'Brentwood is at least an hour on and Colchester two hours back.' He hung down his head into his hands and looked across at the three figures opposite, his face curling into fear as he saw the dead passenger.

'If they think that this is my fault, I'll lose me job and if that happens…'

'The right wheel feathered from its axle. It would take an inspector two minutes to ascertain such damage and I can attest to your good skill in driving should the need arise.'

'And who might you be, sir?'

'Taris Wellingham.'

Beatrice thought she had never heard a more interesting name. Taris. She turned the unusual name over in her mind as the driver rattled on.

'The next packet won't be along till after dawn even should we fail to arrive in Brentwood. They will think in this weather we have sheltered in Ingatestone or stopped further back at Great Baddow. By morning we will all be in the place that he has gone to.' His hand gestured to the passenger opposite, but he stopped when the old woman started to wail.

'It will not come to that, madam.' Taris Wellingham broke into her cries. 'I have already promised to ride on.'

'Not alone, sir.' Beatrice surprised herself with such an outburst, but in these climes a single misstep could mean the difference between life and death and a companion could counter at least some of that danger. 'Besides, I am a good horsewoman.' Or had been, she thought, fifteen years ago in the countryside around Norwich.

'There is no promise that we will make the destination, madam,' he returned, 'and so any such thing is out of the question.'

But Bea stood firm. 'How many horses are there?'

'Four, although one is lame.'

'I am not a child, sir, and if I have a desire to accompany you to the next town and a horse is available for me, then I can see no reason why you should be dictating the terms.'

'You could die if you come.'

'Or die here if you fail to come back.'

'This is a busy road...'

'Upon which we have not seen another vehicle since the journey was resumed after luncheon.'

He smiled, the warmth in his face seen even through the gloom surprising her into a blush. 'It would be dangerous.'

'Less so with the two of us.'

'I'll take the driver with me, then.'

'Both his hands are broken, sir. Surely you can see the angle of his fingers. He is going nowhere!'

Silence greeted her last outburst, but she heard him draw in a careful breath and just as carefully expel it.

'What are you called?' The imperiousness of his tone brought to mind a man who seldom had to wait for anything.

'Mrs Bassingstoke. Mrs Beatrice-Maude Bassingstoke.' She never felt happy giving her name and this occasion was no different, though the eyes that watched her did not fill with the more usual amusement. Nay, rather they seemed to focus above her and away as if he were already plotting their journey.

'Very well, Mrs Bassingstoke. Do you have other clothes in your bag?'

'I do, sir.'

'Then I should take them from where you have them and dress in as many layers as you can manage.' He passed the fabric she had given him a few moments earlier back. 'You will need this shawl for your neck.'

'It is a muslin cloth, sir. From around the cake.'

He hesitated. 'In lieu of a scarf it will do.'

Damn it, Taris thought, the thing had felt just like a woman's scarf. Sometimes the sharpness of touch deserted him as fully as sight did and he had heard a questioning note in the voice of this Beatrice-Maude Bassingstoke.

Her voice did not suit the hardness of her name though in its careful cadence he fancied he heard the whisper of secrets.

Bassingstoke? A Norfolk family and she had made mention of Brampton. He had heard something only last month about them, though he could not quite remember what. Would this woman hail from the same bloodline? The quiet strength in her voice had helped him with everything and she had not eaten any of the cake when he had failed to understand what it was she was offering and did not reach out. Even now the small scent of raisins and rum permeated the air and he wished he might have asked her to open her bag again and cut him a slice.

The thought made him smile, though in truth there was very little humour in their situation. If a carriage or a horseman did not pass by soon he would need to get going himself, for the breathing of the older woman was becoming more shallow, a sign that the cold was getting to her. At least the lady next to him seemed determined to accompany him and for that he was glad. He would need a set of good eyes on the frozen road, one that could see even a glimmer of light in any of the fields, denoting a farmhouse or a barn. In this cold any help was gratifying. He had looked for his own luggage outside but could not glean even a shape of it in the snow. Indeed, the carriage had dragged along for a good few seconds before it had tipped and his case might be anywhere. A pity! The clothes inside it would have been an extra layer that he would have to do without, though with the driver recovered he could ask for his cloak to be returned at least.

He listened to the rustle of Beatrice-Maude Bassingstoke dressing, her arm against his as she wriggled into the extra layers. A thin arm, he realised, the bones of it fragile.

Finally she seemed ready. He wanted to ask her if she had a hat on. He wanted to know if her boots were sturdy. He voiced none of these questions, however, deciding that silence was the wiser option and that Mrs Bassingstoke seemed, even on such a short acquaintance, a rather determined woman and one sensible enough to wrap herself up warm against the elements.

Chapter Two

The weather had worsened when they slipped outside half an hour later, Taris Wellingham carefully replacing the door and patting wads of snow in the gaps that he felt along both edges.

Bea was relieved in a sense to be away from the carriage and doing something, the wait almost worse in the extreme cold than this concerted push of energy, though her heartbeat rose with the fear of being swirled away by the wind and lost into greyness.

As if he could read her mind his hand reached out and clamped across her own, pulling her with him towards the horses, who were decidedly jumpy.

His fingers skimmed across the head of the big grey nearest to him, and down the side to the leather trace, hardened by ice.

'You take this one.'

He held his hand out as a step, and she quickly mounted, abandoning propriety to ride astride. Gathering the reins in tight, she stepped the horse away from the tree. Her hat was a godsend, the wide brim gathering flakes and giving her some respite from the storm. She watched as Taris Wellingham gained his seat and turned the horse towards her, his cloak once again in place and the hat of the younger man jammed in a strange manner down across his ears.

'We'll ride south.'

Away from the direction they had come, which was a sensible choice given the lack of any buildings seen for miles.

Please, God, let there be a house or a barn or travellers who knew the way well. Please, please let us find a warm and safe place and men who could rescue the others. Her litany to an ever-present and omnipotent deity turned over and over, the echoes of other unanswered prayers she had offered up over the years slightly disturbing.

No, she should not think such thoughts, for only grateful vassals of the Lord would be listened to. Had not Frankwell told her that? Squinting her eyes against the driving snow, she lay low across the horse, the warmth of its skin giving her some respite from the cold and she kept her mind very carefully blank.

Quarter of an hour later she knew she could go no further. Everything was numb. Taris Wellingham on the horse beside her looked a lot less uncomfortable, though she knew him to have on fewer clothes than she did. A man used to the elements and its excesses, she supposed.

A man who strode through his life with the certainty that only came with innate self-assurance. So unlike her!

When the shapes of two travellers on horses loomed out of the swirling whiteness she could barely believe them to be real.

'There…in front of us…' she shouted, pointing at them and amazed that Taris Wellingham had as not yet reacted to the sighting. The shout of the newcomers was heard and they waited in silence as the men came abreast.

'The coach from Colchester is late. We have been sent to find it. Are you some of that party?'

'We are, but it is a good fifteen minutes back,' Taris shouted. 'The wheel sheared away…'

'And the passengers?'

'One dead and two more lie inside with the driver, who is badly injured.'

The other man swore.

'Fifteen minutes back, you say. We will have to take them over to Bob Winter's place for the night, then, but that's another twenty or so minutes from here and you look as if you may not be able to stand the journey.'

'What of the old Smith barn?' the other yelled. 'The hay is in and the walls are sturdy.'

'Where is it?' Taris Wellingham sounded tired, the gash on his head still seeping and new worry filled her.

'Five minutes on from here is a path to the left marked with a white stone. Turn there and wait for help. We will send it when we can.'

When we can? The very thought had Bea's ire running.

'I cannot…'

But the others were gone, spurred on by the wind and by need and by the thick white blankets of snow.

'It's our only chance,' Taris shouted, a peal of thunder underlining his reason. The next flash of lightning had her horse rearing up and though she managed to remain seated, the jolt worsened the ache of her lip. Tears pooled in her eyes, scalding hot down her cheeks, the only warmth in the frozen waste of the world.

'I'm sorry.' She saw him looking, his expression so unchanged she knew instantly that he was one of those men who loathed histrionics.

'Look for the pathway, Mrs Bassingstoke. We just need to find the damn barn.'

Prickly. High-handed. Disdainful.

Dashing her tears away with the wet velvet of her cloak, she hated the fact that she had shown any man such weakness. Again.

The path was nowhere. No stone to mark it, no indent where feet might have travelled, no telltale breakage in the hedges to form a track or furrows in the road where carts might have often travelled.

'Are you looking?'

Lord, this was the fifth time he had asked her that very question and she was running out of patience. She wondered why he had dismounted and was leading his steed, his feet almost in the left-hand ditch on the road. Feeling with his feet. For what? What did he search for? Why did he not just ride, fast in the direction they had been shown?

She knew the answer even as she mulled it over. It was past five minutes and if they had missed the trail…?

Suddenly an avenue of trees loomed up.

'Here! It is here!'

He turned into the wind and waited.

'Where? What do you see?'

'Trees. In a row. Ten yards to the left.'

The stone was where the travellers had said it would be, but covered in snow it was barely visible, a marker that blended in with its background, alerting no one to the trail it guarded.

When Taris Wellingham's feet came against it she saw the way he leant over, brushing the snow from the top in a strangely guarded motion, the tips of his fingers purple with the extreme and bitter cold. The stillness in him was dramatic, caught against the blowing trees and the moving landscape and the billowing swirls of his cloak. A man frozen in just this second of time, the hard planes of his face angled to the heavens as though in prayer.

Thank the Lord they had found the barn, Taris thought, and squinted against the cold, trying to see the vestige of a pathway, his eyes watering with the effort.

Beatrice-Maude Bassingstoke's teeth behind him chattered with an alarming loudness, though she had not spoken to him for the last few moments.

'Are you able to make it to the barn?' he asked, the concern in his voice mounting.

'O…of c…c…course I c…c…can.'

'If you need any help…?'

'I sh…shan't.' Tears were close.

'Are you always so prickly, Mrs Bassingstoke?' Anger was easier to deal with than distress and with experience Taris had come to the realisation that a bit of annoyance gave women strength.

But this one was different, her silence punctuated now with sniffs, hidden he supposed by the muffled sound behind the thick velvet of her cloak.

A woman at the very end of her tether and who could blame her? She had not sat in the coach expecting others to save her or bemoaned the cold or the accident. She had not complained about the deceased passenger or made a fuss when she had had to vacate her seat to allow the driver some space. No, this woman was a lady who had risen to each difficulty with the fortitude of one well able to cope. Until now. Until an end was in sight, a warm barn with the hope of safety.

He had seen such things before in the war years in Europe, when soldiers after a battle had simply gone to pieces, the fact that they had remained unscathed whilst so many others had perished around them pushing them over the edge.

A place where Beatrice-Maude Bassingstoke seemed to have reached.

He wished he could have scanned her face for a clue as to her state of well-being, but with only the near-silent sniffles he had little to go on.

How much further to go, he wondered, the snow deepening in the trail with every passing step, though an eddy in the wind against his face told him that a building must be near, the breeze passing over an edifice and rising.

His own awareness of the proximity of objects kicked in too, his cursed lack of sight honing other senses. Placing his hand against the solidness of wood, he thanked God for their deliverance and reached out for the bridle of his companion's horse.

'I will help you down.'

'Th…thank y…you.'

Her hand came to his shoulder as he lifted his arms, fitting them around a waist that was worryingly thin. When he had her down she held on to him still, her fingers entwined in the cloth of his cape.

'I c…can't feel my f…feet,' she explained when he tilted his head in question.

'Then I'll carry you.' Hoisting her against him, he walked a few paces around the edge of the building, finding it open on the southern side, the horses following them in.

The smell of hay and silage was strong and another smell too. Chickens, he thought, listening for the tell-tale sound of scratching. Perhaps there might be eggs or grain here.

Taris liked the feeling of Beatrice-Maude's breath against his collarbone, the warm shallowness of it a caress that surprised him. How old was this lady? When her hand rested against the smoothness of his skin, he felt a band of gold on the third finger of her left hand.

Worry engulfed him. Would her husband be mad with worry somewhere?

'I c...can s...see that th...there are bl...blankets in the f...far corner, I th...think. Perhaps we c...could w...warm ourselves.'

Which corner? In the gloom of his vision Taris could detect nothing save the walls enclosing this space. Another thought heartened him. Perhaps if he let her down she might lead him to them.

When her feet touched the dirt floor Beatrice winced, the numbness now replaced by a pins-and-needles pain that made contact with anything unbearable. She could never in her whole life remember feeling this cold, the sheer pain of it seeping into her bones and making her heavy and sluggish. She almost crawled to the corner, glad to finally be off her feet; removing her boots, she burrowed into the warmth of a scratchy grey horse blanket.

But her clothes were wet and stiff and the cold that she thought might disappear suddenly increased with the change in circumstance.

Taris Wellingham at her side was peeling off his cloak, and the wet steamy shirt he had on followed it.

She looked away, her breath indrawn by the tone of muscle, the shaped contours attesting to the fact that he must spend much of his life out of doors.

'Take your cloak off too,' he said as he jumped under her blanket and heaped his cloak on top.

'Wh…what are you d…doing?' Panic lent a screeching sound to the query.

'One can die of the cold in a matter of moments. Skin to skin we can warm each other.'

'Sk…in to skin?' Lord, that he should even suggest such a thing.

'Feel this,' he returned and placed her hand across her throat. A clammy coldness emanated from her, the beat of her heart beneath shallow and fast.

'And then feel this.'

Now her fingers lay against his chest, the hair tickling her palm. But it was his heat that got to her, a blazing hotness that seemed to cover each and every part of him.

She could not pull away, could not make herself remember manners and propriety and comportment. All she wanted was to be closer and when he helped her take the cloak from her shoulders she did nothing to dissuade him.

'How old are you?' he said above the silence.

'Tw…twenty-eight.'

'And your husband?'

'Is d…dead.'

'Then I have no need to be concerned that an avenging swain will appear and challenge me to a duel.'

'No, sir. It is only your w…warmth that I w…want.'

'Good.' His response was measured and brisk, her worries about anything more between them singularly ridiculous in the whole situation.

Of course he would not want more from her! She bent

her head so that he might not see her blush. Lord, the thinness of her arms against his healthy shape was unattrac-tive and her dress with the long sleeves was as wet as his shirt.

'Take this off, too.'

'I will n…not.'

In response he simply sat her up and unbuttoned the gown before slipping it from her. In the darkness she saw that the livid red scar near her elbow was difficult to make out. Still when his fingers touched the skin they lingered, his question of how this had happened almost a physical thing in the gloom.

'I f…fell against a f…fence.'

'And it was not tended?'

'The doctor tried his hardest…'

A sharp bark of laughter confused her. Not humorous in any way. Just harsh. Critical.

Her stays and chemise and petticoat beneath were a little damp and she was pleased he did not insist she take them off too. She noticed after removing his boots he left his own trousers on, the wet fabric catching on the skin of her legs as they laid themselves down.

Together. Spooned. His back against her face. She could not help her hands wandering to the warmth.

'Will the h…horses b…be s…safe?'

'They will keep warm together if they have any sense.'

'You h…have d…done this before? B…been caught in the s…snow, I mean?' Lord, the clumsiness of her question made her stiffen. Of course he would have lain with a woman. Many women probably, with his fine face and his courage!

He did not seem to notice her faltering as he answered her question. 'I fought in Europe in the Second Peninsular campaign and it often was colder there than in England. The men were not as soft as you are, though, when we lay down at night.' A smile was audible in his voice.

A personal compliment! Bea left the edge of awkwardness alone and thought about other things: the sound of the horses nuzzling in, the snow outside, and a wind that howled through the rafters of the roof. All things to keep her mind off a growing realisation that the warmth was no longer concentrated solely in him.

To lie with a man in a snow-filled night, safe after adversity, a man who was neither sickly nor mean. A man with a man's body, a man's tastes, the smell of his skin woody and strong, his muscles even in the dimness defined and substantive.

So unlike Frankwell.

Years of celibacy suddenly weighed against opportunity; the widow Bassingstoke was presented with a fine handsome man and a night that would hold no questions.

The ghost of a smile played around her lips before sense reined it in. Of course she could not take advantage of the situation. She was a lady and a widow. Besides, already she thought his body had relaxed into sleep, the even cadence of his breath confirming it. To him she was nothing more than a warm skin to survive against. When the tip of her finger reached out to the ridge of his shoulder blade and traced the muscle in air, she wished that she might have been braver and truly touched him.

So unwise, another voice cautioned, the knowledge of her plainness leading only to a rejection that would be embarrassing to them both.

He came awake with a start. Where the hell was he? A leg lay across his stomach. A shapely leg by the feel of it, fully exposed almost up to the groin.

His groan took him by surprise, his manhood rising without any help from his mind.

Lord. Mrs Beatrice-Maude Bassingstoke had a sensuality about her that was elemental. He had not felt it before with his tiredness and his worry, but here with the first slam of awareness he was knocked for six. It lay in her smell and the breath of trust against his chest. It lingered in the hair uncoiled from the tight knot he had felt before finding sleep and which now curtained across him, thick and curly. The line of her breasts too was surprising. The thinness of her waist and of her arms was not mirrored here, her fat abundance of soft womanhood moulded against him, her nipples through thin lawn grazing his own with a surprising result.

God. His erection had grown again, filling the space of his trousers with warmth and promise. God, he muttered once more as she moved in sleep, this time all but crawling on top of him in her quest for warmth. His sex nudged at her thighs and he did not stop it, the very sensation tightly bound up in the forbiddenness of the situation.

A quandary he had no former experience of. A stranger who seduced him even in her sleep, the smell of her wafting beneath his nose. Flowers and woman.

And trust. A powerful aphrodisiac in a man who had forgotten the emotion, forgotten the very promise of intimate closeness!

He opened his eyes as widely as he could, trying to catch in them a reflection of light. Any light. But the darkness was complete, the snow and wind blocking moonbeams with the time, by his reckoning, being not much past the hour of two.

The witching hour. The hour he usually prowled the confines of his house away from the stares of others, darkness overcoming disability and all of the lights turned down.

Here, however, he did not wish to rise. Here he wanted to stay still, and just feel. The incline of her chest, the tremor in her hands as if a dream might have crept into her slumber, the feel of her hair wound around his fingers, clamping him to her.

His!

This thin and sensible lass, with her twenty-eight years and her widowhood.

Was it recent? Had her husband just died, the ring she wore a reminder of all the happy years she now would never enjoy? Were there children? Did she rule a domain of offspring and servants with her sense and sensibility? A woman at the centre of her world and with no need for any other? Certainly not for a man with fading sight and the quickening promise of complete blindness!

His arousal flagged slightly, but regained ground when her fingers clamped on his own, anchoring her to him. A ship in a storm, and any port welcomed.

He could not care. The rush of desire and need was unlike any he had ever experienced. He needed to take her, to possess her, to feel the softness of her flesh as he pushed inside to be lost in warmth.

He rocked slightly, guilt buried beneath want. And then he rocked again.

Chapter Three

She felt the bud of excitement, the near promise of something she had never known. Breathing in, she whispered a name.

'*Taris.*'

His name.

The answering curse pulled her fully awake, his face close, the darkness of it lightened by the line of his teeth as he spoke.

'Beatrice-Maude? Is there a name that you are called other than that? It is long, after all, and I thought—'

'Bea.' She broke into his words with a whisper. 'My mother always called me Bea.'

'Bea,' he repeated, turning the name over on his tongue and she felt his breath against her face as he said it. So close, so very close. He held his hand across her waist when she tried to pull back.

'Bea as in Bea-witching?'

His fingers trailed down her cheek, warm and real.

'Or Bea as in Bea-utiful?'

She tensed, waiting for his laugh, but it did not come.

'Hardly that, sir.' She felt the heavy thrump of her heartbeat in her throat. Was he jesting with her? Was he a man who lied in order to receive what he wanted, who thought such untruthful inanities the desperate fodder expected by very plain women? She tried to turn from him to find a distance, the sheer necessity of emotional survival paramount.

'What is it? What is wrong?' A thread of some uncertainty in his voice was the only thing that held her in place. If she had heard condescension or falsity she would have stood, denying his suggestion of more, even knowing that she might never in her whole life be offered anything as remotely tempting.

Again.

'I should rather honesty, sir.'

'Sir?' The word ended in a laugh. 'Surely "sir" is too formal for the position we now find ourselves in?' He did not take back his compliments and another bark of laughter left her dazed.

'Are you a celibate widow, Mrs Beatrice-Maude Bassingstoke?'

She started to nod and then changed her mind, not sure of exactly what he alluded to.

'Then I suppose there is another question I must ask of you. Are you a woman who would say nay to the chance of sharing more than just warmth together here in the midst of a storm?'

His voice was silken smooth, a tone in it that she could not quite fathom.

Her brows knitted together. 'I don't understand.'

He pushed inwards and the hardness of his sex made everything crystal clear.

A dalliance. A tryst. One stolen and forbidden night. For twelve years she had wondered what it would be like to lie with a man who was not greedy or selfish. A man who might consider her needs as well as his own. Always lovemaking had hurt her; he had hurt her when she had tried to take her pleasure in the act. Frankwell Bassingstoke and his angry punitive hands.

What would Taris Wellingham's touch be like, his slender fingers finding places she had only ever dreamed about?

Lord, but to dare to take the chance of one offered providence and the end of it come morning.

No strings attached, no empty unfilled promises to lie awake and worry over come the weeks and months that followed. Only these hours, the darkness sheltering anything she did not wish him to see. And then an ending.

Twenty-eight and finally free. The heady promise of it was as exhilarating as it was unexpected.

'You mean this for just one night only?'

She needed to understand the parameters of such a request, for if he said he wanted more she would know that he lied and know also that she should not want it.

'Yes.'

Freedom. Impunity. Self-government and her own reign.

Words that had been the antithesis of all she had been for the past twelve years and words that she vowed would shape her life for all of those still to come.

Her husband's face hovered above her, his heavy frown and sanctimonious nature everything that she had hated. At sixteen she had not been old enough to recognise the faults and flaws of a man who would become her husband, but at twenty-eight she certainly did.

He had been a bully, an oppressive domineering tyrant and with his bent for religious righteousness she had never quite been able to counter any of it.

She shook her head hard. Nay, all that was over. Now she would do only as she wanted so long as it did not harm any other.

'Are you married?'

Her question was blurted out. If he said that he was, she would not touch him.

'No.'

Permission granted. Placing her hand flat on his chest, her forefinger found his nipple. With deliberation she lent down and wet it with her tongue, blowing on the cold as she caressed it into rigidity.

When he stretched out and groaned she felt the control of a woman with power. Feminine power, the feeling unlike any she had ever experienced.

She did not feel guilty as Frankwell had said that she must, she did not feel sullied or soiled or befouled. Nay, she felt the sheer and utter wonder of it, the bewildering rarity of rightness.

Here. With Taris Wellingham. For this one storm-snowed freezing night.

'Thank you.' The words slipped out without recognition as to what she had said. A beholden contentment that broke through all that she had believed of herself or all that a husband steeped in damning religion had believed. In just one touch Frankwell's hold on the tenure of her moral pureness was gone, replaced simply by comprehension and relief.

She smiled as his fingers began to unlace her bodice and the thin lawn fell away.

'Thank you?'

The restraint that Taris was trying to hold in check broke, the swollen want between them demanding nothing hidden or reserved. Running his fingers down the curve of her arm, he gathered the ties on her lacy chemise and unravelled them, her face tipping up to his own.

He imagined her eyes, surprise and lust in equal measure; he imagined her mouth, the feel of her lips full and tender. When his hands cupped her breasts and held the flesh in his palms, he took a shaky breath out, for this woman did not wait for him to do all the work. No, already her fingers skimmed the waistband of his trousers, slipping into the skin that lay underneath and feeling his erection with as much care and vigilance as he was giving to her.

A balanced taking.

No missish virgin or paid whore. No money between them or commitment sought. Only feelings.

'Ahhh, Beatrice-Maude,' he whispered as she pushed the material covering him downwards and her fingers came to other places, more hidden. No green or frightened girl either.

Equal measure!

Touch for touch! Stopping only as his mouth fastened upon her nipple and tasted, the sweet sound of bliss in her voice as she expelled her breath and enjoyed.

The dampness of her skin, and her stark utter heat. The way her hips rocked against his own, asking, wanting, needing more.

His head rose to her mouth, and his fingers felt the way, her chin, her nose, the lay of her eyes and her forehead. No colour but shape, and crowned with a pile of darkened curls. That much at least he could see!

'Let me take you, sweetheart. Let me take you further.' His voice did not seem like his own.

'Yes,' she answered. 'Much further...'

Her heavy breasts swayed as he brought her up with him, the fall of her legs opening beneath her chemise. His hand crept under it to her stockings, which he removed, and then to her drawers, lacy pieces of nothing, the un-sewn seam leaving easy access.

'Now,' she cried and not quietly either. 'Right now.' The sweat between them built, the cold of this barn a far-off thought, no time for careful restraint or the foreplay that he was more used to. No time for any of it as he lifted her on to him and drove home, again and again and again, a life-filled, raw loving that was all that was left to seek release.

Which they did!

She had died and gone to heaven! She swore she had. She swore that if her life were to end now, this very, very minute she would leave a happy woman. A fulfilled woman. A woman who finally knew what it was novels spoke of in their flurry of adjectives and superlatives.

This. Feeling.

Spent and replete and waves of ecstasy still sweeping across her. And tears when she began to cry.

Not quietly either. But loudly. Loud tears of wonderment and relief. She just could not stop them.

'Did I hurt you? Are you hurt?'

She waved away his worry and tried to smile.

'No. It was wonderful. So wonderful.' Bruised with happiness and finality. Understanding what it was she had not experienced before.

He lay back against the scratchy grey blanket in the year's new hay and began to laugh.

'You are crying…because it was wonderful?'

She nodded, the sniffs now lessened as she sought for her chemise balled beside them in order to blow her nose.

'I didn't know…' no, she could tell him none of her past for she did not want him feeling sorry for her '…that a hay barn could be such a sensual place.'

Before her he lay like a prince devoid of clothes and inhibitions. A Greek god fallen into her lap by the will of a Lord who had finally answered her daily prayers.

A whole twelve years of them to be precise, and not more than a month after the death of Frankwell Bassingstoke!

Perhaps that was all the time needed for a powerful deity to recognise the sacrifice she had made to care for her given husband, to obey him, to yield to the orders he had been so fond of giving.

Perhaps Taris Wellingham had been sent in recompense, the gift of this night easily making up for the hardship of her past decade.

His finger traced the upward turn of her lips.

'You are a puzzle, Mrs Bassingstoke,' he said, his voice rich with the rounded vowels of a well-to-do upbringing. 'And one that I cannot, for the life of me, quite fathom.'

She stayed silent, enjoying his touch as he splayed open her palm and drew a spiral inside before tracing upwards to the sensitive folds of her neck and the outline of her lips.

When his hand cupped the back of her nape and he pulled her down across him she went willingly, his mouth taking what she offered in a hard twist of desire. Seeking. Finding. The taste of him masculine and fierce, though for the first time she was frightened, frightened of the need that welled in her, wanting, wishing this was real and binding her to eternity.

'No.' She pulled back and he did not stop her, did not hurt her in his insistence or his demand. Actions so unlike Frankwell that her fear subsided.

'I should not exact anything you do not wish to offer.'

Quiet words from an honourable man, his need felt easily against her stomach, yet still he gave her the choice.

Her head dipped down and she ran her tongue across his lips, her fingers splayed against his chest as she held him still.

As if sensing her need for control, he remained motionless even as her touch cupped the full hardness of him.

'My turn now,' she whispered and stroked his warmth, teasing as he writhed. 'Not yet,' she added as he moved up against her. 'Or yet,' she repeated as she sat astride him and guided the fullness to a place that was only hers to offer. Home. Replete. Abundant. 'But now.'

The feel of him made her tip back her head and cry out his name, no longer quiet as her voice broke against the wind and the rain and the wild sound of trees. The storm of sex was now inside her too, reaching, reaching and breaking languid sweet in her belly, her fingers and toes stretched tight against the ripples, urging them on for longer, unfastened by any ties of right or wrong.

Only feeling.

Only them.

When the last of the contractions had ceased she lay against him, joined by flesh and the slick wetness of their lovemaking. His hand claimed her, lying over her bottom, skin to skin, the cold air diminishing their heat. The length of her tresses was bound in his other fist, fettered in nakedness, lost in the glory.

'Bea?' Whispered.

'Yes.' Whispered back.

'Bea-yond anything.'

Her laughter took his body from her own.

This was what she had missed all of her life. Just this. No meanness in it or bad temper. No righteous lecture on the innate evil of all women's nature.

Beyond. Anything.

When his fingers crept into the space his body had just left, she opened her legs wide and all that was wonderful before began again.

She was asleep. Catching dreams from the early dawn. He did not wish to wake her, but he had to, for the winds had fallen and the sky was lightening. At least that much he could see and feel. They would be here soon. Everybody. The world. Reality.

The sun and the light and the damming affliction of his soul.

He would not be able to see her. He did not know the lay of this barn, the traps and the pitfalls. And she would know all of what he wasn't, so carefully hidden in the dark.

His breathing shallowed and the fear that he had lived with for three years thickened. This time it did matter. Mrs Beatrice-Maude Bassingstoke and her generous soft body even now in sleep turned towards him and wanting. Again.

He could not take her. He could not risk it with the new day dawning over a weakening storm. The blood that ran to the place between his legs did not listen to his head, however.

Once more, please the Lord, time for just once more.

She was wet and willing and pliable and, seeking entry with his hands, he knew the second she awakened, bearing down upon him as she guided him in.

The dawn was now well and truly broken and Taris dressed with haste before walking carefully around the shelter and marking its shape. Thirty yards long and twenty across, the haystack in the corner reaching out a considerable distance. The rough-sawn timber the barn was built with left a splinter in his palm and, sucking it hard, he saw the movements of Beatrice-Maude dressing. He hoped that she had tidied her hair and removed the traces of straw from her clothes that he had felt when he had brushed against them. He did not move back towards her, however, but turned to the open end of the building, tilting his head so that he could hear the sounds from further off.

They were coming.

People were coming.

Binding his hair into a tight queue, he stood with his face against the sky and waited, the hat that he had borrowed from the younger man in the carriage pulled down across his forehead, shading his eyes from other prying ones.

'A rescue party will be here in five minutes,' he warned, his voice distant. He could not help it. This was a place he had no knowledge of and the daylight was upon them. If he walked towards her, he might trip on a misplaced object and his brother had described to him in detail the opaque clouds in his left eye.

He did not wish for Beatrice-Maude Bassingstoke to see that. He did not want her to know that he was a man who functioned best only in the darkness, a man who depended on his trusted servants and the familiar shore-lines of his home. Risk free and easy.

'You can hear them?' she asked and he merely nodded. 'Well, I can make out nothing at all and I always thought myself rather accomplished on hearing things that others could not.'

She sounded nervous and a little desperate, the higher tones of a frantic embarrassment clearly audible.

Why?

She was a widow after all and far from her first flush of youth and the night they had spent together had been completely consensual.

Perhaps it was the sheer worry of having others come to judge her in the predicament she now found herself in, for co-habiting overnight with a man would be considered racy even in his circle of friends and Mrs Bassingstoke sounded more like someone at home in the country.

His fist beat against his thigh as he pondered options. 'I will disclose our sleeping arrangements to no one, Mrs Bassingstoke. Perhaps that will put your mind at rest.'

'Indeed, Mr Wellingham.' He was bothered by the worry in her words. Hardly above a whisper.

'And if you could be so good as to fashion a nest in the hay that would only leave room for one person, then that should help this charade further.'

He listened as she did as he had suggested before sliding down to sit against the wall. Two people sheltering at either end of the barn and fully clothed! He hated the small catch he could hear in her voice as she began to talk again.

'Are you based in London, sir?'

He shook his head. 'More often than not I am away from it,' he returned.

'I see.' He heard the deep intake of breath as she contemplated his answer. 'So if by chance I should catch sight of you in the streets…?'

'Your reputation would stay safer should you ignore me altogether.'

'Ignore you altogether.'

Echoed. Lonely. Taris wished he might take his words back and replace them with other, softer words, words that did not decimate any contact with such a final thrust. But there was nothing he could do, not here, caught at the mercy of everyone, a man who was not able to even find his way to the edge of a small barn without falling.

His rejoinder cut into the quick of Bea's self-esteem. Of course he would not wish for a plain woman of little attraction to be vying for his attention. Questions would be asked, after all, and she was hardly the sort who would be able to shrug them off with an inconsequential ease.

Ever since waking this morning he had barely glanced her way. Once had been enough, probably, to determine her mousy-coloured hair and her unremarkable eyes, let alone a nose that was hardly retroussé and a chin that was much more defiant than was deemed fashionable.

Plain!

She had never felt the condition with such an agony and the ache of rejection was wretched. Taking a breath, she tried to exhale in a calm and dignified manner. Frankwell might have robbed her of youth, but a will that had been long bent was again firming, and the gift of independence was something that she could cling to. She had both gold and land and the means to be beholden to no one. Ever again! It was at least a start.

Swallowing, she stood, the group of people coming on horseback now visible, the men they had spoken to last night joined by a good many others, society folk, their dress rich and ornate.

When they finally came within ten yards of the barn the most beautiful woman Beatrice had ever seen in her life slid from her steed and ran.

'Taris. Taris. Oh, thank God.' Her eyes were flooded with tears and the chignon in its net had slipped, allowing a halo of blonde silken curls to fall in riotous abandon down to her shoulders as she flung herself into his opened arms.

'My God, we thought we…had lost you…we thought you had been swept away in the storm or buried beneath the pile of snow and the hailstones…have you ever seen such hailstones…?'

The tirade stopped only as turquoise eyes came level with Bea's, interest stamped across uncertainty.

Taris Wellingham turned finally in her direction, his amber gaze running quickly over her as though only just remembering that she was indeed still here. 'Emerald Wellingham, meet Mrs Beatrice-Maude Bassingstoke.'

Emerald Wellingham?

He was married? My God, he had lied to her, lied about everything…

'She is my sister-in-law.'

Relief made the world bend in a strange way and Bea placed her hand against the wall to steady herself. Taris Wellingham neither came forwards nor commented on her instability and the callous indifference in his eyes confirmed her deductions. She meant nothing to him. She was just a warm and docile body with whom a freezing night had been passed more quickly. But at least he was not married!

She felt the turquoise gaze of the newcomer take in her dishevelled clothes and the hay that was stuck to them, summing up her character in the clues that lay all around.

A plain woman who would take the chance of an unexpected night with a man who looked as beautiful as this one did.

Shame battled with anger and both were overtaken by surprise as another man with a look of menacing danger joined them. Beatrice noticed he had a rather pronounced limp.

'We travelled up from London at first light when you failed to come to Park Avenue. Emerald had a feeling about it all and would not be fobbed off with any excuse.'

'It was the storms that made me uneasy, Taris, though Asher said I should not be concerned...'

Asher and Taris Wellingham? The names were suddenly horrifyingly familiar to Beatrice, for she had read of them across the years, two brothers who had ruled the *ton* with their wealth and escapades.

Falder Castle was their seat and they were the direct descendants of the first Duke of Carisbrook and if memory served her well Taris Wellingham had recently acquired extensive properties in Kent. Her cheeks burned with the growing realisation of how far she had trespassed into a world she knew nothing of and all she wanted was to be gone from this place, removed to one of the carriages that she could see now pulling up to the barn, further faces turned towards her, questions in their eyes.

'The weather will be upon us in the next few moments, my lord, if we do not hurry from here.' A tall thin man had come to the side of Taris Wellingham and she was bemused by the way he threaded his arm through that of his master.

The woman Emerald seemed as protective, her hand coming into his on the other side as they turned for the coach. She was amazed that Taris Wellingham allowed them to shepherd him in such a manner and was about to say something when his brother gave an order to the servant next to her.

'See to the woman, Forbes.' The young servant nodded even as the Wellinghams disappeared from view.

She could not believe it. He would not even tarry to say goodbye after all that they had shared?

The sound of a door shutting and a call to the horses answered her query. Then the beat of hooves and a quickening pace, the contraption lost to the whiteness of the landscape and the newly falling snow.

Gone.

Finished.

'If you would come this way, miss, the others are in the coach...'

'Others?'

There was a shout of recognition from the old woman and her son she had met the night before as she scrambled up the steps and into the shelter of the vehicle. She was pleased to find no sign of the one who had been killed in the accident. Or the driver.

'Mr Brown was taken on to London an hour or so ago and the other went to Brentwood to the church, I would guess, until his family have been notified to collect him.' The younger man was full of chatter, his mother less talkative after such a long and harrowing night.

'We spent the night at a farmhouse further north and were picked up just a little time ago. He's brother to a Duke, you know, the man we all rode with, and he has a wealth of land in Kent.'

Bea nodded, pleased when the carriage was spurred on, the droning sound of miles being eaten up as they travelled south sending the others to sleep.

Lord Taris Wellingham, brother to the Duke of Carisbrook.

She turned the names on her tongue, grand names, names that were known in all the four corners of this country, the lineage of the dukedom reaching down through a thousand years of privilege and entitlement.

Taris Wellingham.

She remembered his profile turned against the snow, strong and proud, a man who might not understand how easily he intimidated others with his effortless leadership and control.

Control over the reactions of her body too, every bit as persuasive yet infinitely gentle.

'Enough,' she whispered into the gathering greyness of the morning and, pulling the collar of her cloak around her eyes, she was glad to hide her tears from a world that she no longer understood.

Taris felt his sister-in-law's gaze on him even as he turned to the window, looking out.

Lord, he was a coward and a faint-heart and as the miles between them grew he understood something he had never in his life before experienced.

A woman had bettered him, had made him feel a cad of the very first order, a man who would not own up to either circumstance or reality, but hid in a world that was only deception.

'So if by chance I should catch sight of you in the streets…?'

'Your reputation would stay safer should you ignore me altogether.'

He took in a breath and held it, hating the tightness he could feel in his throat, loathing the way he still did not say anything.

Turn around. Turn around and go back.

He should say it, should shout it, but with the world only a grey sludge he found that he just could not.

Beatrice-Maude Bassingstoke had seen him at his best. The best that he used to be, before…before he had become dependent on everyone! He wanted her to remember him like that, a man in charge of his life and his actions.

From best to worst, Bates's hand threaded through his own and Emerald's on the other side, leading him out through the space to his carriage. He hoped she had not seen the coat of arms emblazoned on the side or heard Bates calling him 'my lord'. He hoped she might have thought him ill or cold or disorientated. Certainly he hoped that she had not seen him trip as they had rounded the wall of the barn, his feet catching a ditch that he had had no notion was there.

Anger consumed him. And regret. For three years this blindness had been taking his sight day by day and piece by piece. At first it had been just his central vision, but now it was all the light on the periphery too; a creeping silent thief with total blackness as the end point of a journey he had no wish to be making.

A sadness that had been a constant companion of his recent months gathered with biting force, pushing him back in his seat so that his fists almost shook with the sheer and utter wrath of it all.

He had never accepted it, never come to the place where acquiescence might have softened anguish and allowed a healing.

No, he had never come to that!

'Why the hell you insist on these public carriage excursions eludes me, Taris, when you have a bevy of your own conveyances ready and willing to take you anywhere?' Asher's voice sounded wearied and the truth of the query added to Taris's own frustration. This was the first time alone on the road that he had indeed felt sightless, the struggle of coping more overwhelming than it had ever seemed before. He was pleased when his brother took his criticism no further and Emerald spoke instead.

'Your companion sounds interesting?'

'She was.'

'She looked worried, though. I wondered if you had noticed?'

'Yes.'

'I also saw she wore a wedding ring?'

'He's tired, Emmie. Leave him to rest.' Asher's voice wound its way around protection with its particular undercurrent of guilt. Suddenly Taris had had enough.

'Beatrice-Maude Bassingstoke is a widow from Brampton. She is turned twenty-eight. She appreciates honesty and she hates her name.'

'A comprehensive list.' Emerald's voice faltered as Asher began to laugh, and the quick thud of his leg against the side of the coach told Taris of a well-directed kick.

'I thought she seemed...strong.'

'Indeed, she was that.'

'Any woman bold enough to leave the safety of a carriage and venture into a snow-whitened night would win my favour.'

'What does she look like?' Taris had not meant to ask this, so baldly, so very unmindful, and the silence in the carriage was complete until Emerald began to speak again.

'Her hair is the colour of chestnuts ripe in autumn and her eyes hold the hue of wet leaves in the shadows beside a forest stream.'

He stayed silent, hoping that she might carry on, liking the way that she brought Beatrice-Maude to life for him in that peculiar way she had of using words.

'She isn't very tall, but she is very thin. Between her eyes is the line of a woman who has worried a lot. The dimples in her cheeks are the prettiest I have ever seen on anyone.'

Taris nodded, remembering the contours of them, re-membering how she had taken his fingers into her mouth, licking them in the way of one versed in the sensual arts. Remembering other things too. Her smell. Her softness. The whisper of his name against his ear before she had turned into his arms and pressed the swollen flesh of her breasts against him.

'God!' Said without thought.

'What?' Asher's voice was loud, near, edged with perplexity.

Searching around for an excuse, he found one in the missing timepiece at his waist. 'I think I left my watch back under the hay. It was poking against me in the night.'

'Grandpa's fob? You still wear that even though you can't read the numbers?' Asher swore as he registered what it was he had implied.

'Sound measures time as well, brother, and when you stop feeling guilty for my poor eyesight then both of us may sleep all the easier.'

Closing his eyes, Taris liked the ease of not having to try to decipher shapes, though a vision rose in his memory of chestnut curls, leaf-green eyes and smiling dimpled cheeks. And bravery despite heavily chattering teeth!

Beatrice saw Taris Wellingham the following week in Regent Street where she had gone to do some shopping. He was in the passenger seat of an impressive-looking phaeton, a young woman beside him tooling the horses with a confidence that was daunting.

Drawing back against the shop window, she hoped that the overhanging roof might shelter her from his glance should he happen to look her way and her heartbeat was so violent she saw the material in the bodice of her gown rise up and down.

Goodness, would she faint? Already dizziness made her world spin and the maid at her side carrying an assortment of other parcels she had procured looked at her in alarm.

'Are you quite well, ma'am?'

'Certainly, Sarah.' The quiver in her voice was unsettling.

'There is a teahouse just a few shops on if you should care to sit down.'

Across the girl's shoulder Taris Wellingham came closer, his face now easily visible and a top hat that was the height of fashion perched upon his head. The woman beside him was laughing as she urged her horses on and the ordinary folk on the street stopped what they did and watched.

Watched beauty and wealth and privilege. Watched people who had never needed to struggle or count their pennies or wonder where their next meal might come from. Watched a vibrant and beautiful woman handling a set of highly strung greys, which were probably worth their weight in gold, and a man who might let her do so, a smile of pride on his face as she deftly guided them through a busy city throughway.

Bea felt an anger she rarely gave way to as Taris Wellingham's eyes passed right across her own with no acknowledgement or recognition in them.

Just an ill-dressed stranger on a crowded London street watching for a second the passing of the very, very rich. And then dismissed.

Nothing left of breath and touch and the whispered delights shared in a barn outside Maldon. Nothing left of holding the centre of him within her, deep and safe, the snow outside erasing everything that could lead others to them, time skewered only by feelings and trust and the hard burn of an endless want.

Gone! Finished!

She turned her head away and marched into the first shop with an open door, the stocked shelves of a milliner's wares blurring before her eyes as she pretended an exaggerated and determined interest in procuring a hat.

There was no sense in any of this, of course. Had Taris Wellingham not already told her that she should ignore him should she see him in London, that the tryst they had shared was nothing more to him than an interlude in one moment of need? The wedding ring on the third finger of her left hand glinted in the refracted light of a lamp set beside the counter.

Frankwell laughing from the place his soul had been consigned to. Not heaven, she hoped, the religious icon on the wall above the milliner making her start. Would her own actions outside Maldon banish her soul from any hope of an everlasting happiness? Given that she had in all of her twenty-eight years seldom experienced the emotion, the thought made her maudlin, the enticing promise of a better place after such sacrifice the one constant hope in her unending subservience in Ipswich.

Perhaps she was being punished for that very acquiescence, a woman who had been given a brain to think with and who had rarely used it. Was still not using it, was not taking the chances that were suddenly hers to seize, but was hiding away in the shadow of a fear that made everything seem dangerous.

'Is there anything in particular you wish to look at, madam?' the shopkeeper asked, as Bea still did not speak. The silence in the street registered in the back of her mind, any possibility of a further re-encounter diminishing with each passing second.

She made herself look at a hat she had admired on the nearest shelf, touching the soft fabric carefully. The bright green felt was a colour that she had seldom worn, Frankwell's distaste of anything 'showy' in the early years of her marriage mirrored across all of the last.

The very thought of her unquestioned obedience made her try it on, and for the first time ever in her life she actually liked the face of the woman reflected in the mirror. The colour matched her eyes and the tone of her skin, the sallowness of her often-favoured beige or brown lightened by the tint of green.

'I think this colour suits you very well, madam, as would this one.'

A dark red hat replaced the green and the transformation was just as unbelievable.

'I have always worn the shades of colour that are in this gown,' she explained and the woman shook her head forcibly.

'Those tones would not highlight the colour of your eyes, or enhance the cream in your skin.'

She hurried to lift down a creation in beige from a top shelf and brought it back.

'See, madam. This is the colour you have preferred and you can see how little it favours you.'

Beatrice's mouth fell open. Lord. Was it that easy to look more presentable? She could not believe it.

'I have a sister who is just beginning as a modiste in London, madam. If you should wish to consult her for your gowns I am sure she would be very obliging. She is both reasonable and skilled.'

Sarah's head nodded up and down beside her, a wide smile on her face.

Perhaps it was time for a change. A time to look at the things she had always enjoyed in her life and to try to incorporate them in the next part of it.

Books. Ideas. Discussions.

These were the things she had longed for most in the silent big house in Ipswich. When she had tried to speak to Frankwell about her own desires, his set opinions had always overridden her own and his anger had made her wary about disagreeing.

But now? Now that she had the money, time and inclination to follow her own dreams, the colour of a hat that actually suited her took on an importance that even yesterday would have been ridiculous. But here in the aftermath of a galling indifference the worm of something else turned inside her.

Freedom might be possible.

Freedom to do exactly as she pleased and to live her life in a way that would suit her, with no regard to others' opinions.

The thought was heady and thrilling, a mandate to be only as she determined was right for her.

'I will take both hats, please,' she said, pulling out a purse that was filled with money, 'and I should very much like to meet your sister.'

Taris placed his hand across the reins, feeling the pressure.

'Ease up a little on the right, Lucy, for there is a slight pull.'

He knew in the breeze on his face the moment his sister re-aligned the horses and felt a tug of pride.

'You have been practising while I have been away?'

Laughter greeted his question. 'If that is your way of telling me I have improved, brother, then so be it.'

'You have improved.' The words came readily and he felt his sister lay her hand across his own.

'From you that means a lot. All my life I have been in the shadow of my big brothers and it is good to finally cast one of my own. I appreciate the loan of your team in my quest to master this horsemanship, by the way, and if there is ever anything that you would like in return…'

He shook his head. 'Become the Original you are destined to be, Lucinda, and that will be payment enough.'

'Whomever you finally marry will be a lucky lady, Taris, because you have never allowed yourself to define others in the way the *ton* demands. With you I always feel that I could be…anything.'

The wind took his laughter and threw it across the street and in the corner of his vision he could just make out the forms of people watching them.

Women by the looks with their gowns and hats, and the sound of bells pealing out across the afternoon.

Two o'clock. By five he would be on the road south, leaving the traffic and the noise of London behind him. He closed his eyes briefly and imagined the promise of Beaconsmeade and the warm comfort of his home.

He would take his own carriage for the ride down, however, for his recent poor experience with the public transport system allayed the delight he so often felt in mixing with the ordinary folk.

A gentler vision of well-rounded breasts and long dark curls made his fingers clasp with more fervour on to the silver head of his cane. Beatrice-Maude Bassingstoke!

They had both agreed to the limitation of just one night and he had heard the sound of relief in her voice when he had not demanded different. Perhaps the state of widow-hood was more promising than that of Holy Matrimony with its sanctions and its rules. As a man he saw the strictures that a woman was placed under when she married and if she had any land at all...?

No, he could not now search for Bea or betray such a trust. He had no earthly reason for doing so and she did not seem the type of woman who might welcome a dalliance. Besides, a wife was the very last thing he needed with his receding sight and his blurring vision.

Whomever you finally marry will be a lucky lady...

'Your horses are attracting a lot of attention, Taris. Why, nearly everyone is watching their excellence.'

'Well, Lucy, one more round and then home; I have much to do before I depart for Kent.'

'Ash asked you to stay longer.'

'I can't.'

'Or won't.'

Both of them laughed as they careered around the corner and into the pathways of Hyde Park.

Chapter Four

Beatrice tucked her hair behind her ears and surveyed her downstairs salon, bedecked with books on each available surface. Her weekly book discussions were becoming… fashionable, attended by people from every walk of life, a crush that was the talk of the town.

How she loved London, loved its rush and bustle and the way the fabric of life here was so entwined with good debate and politics and culture. No one expected things of her or corrected her. If she wished to spend an evening reading in bed she could. If she wished to go out to a play she could. London with its diversity of intellectual pursuits set her free in a way that she had never been before and she relished such liberty.

Her clothes were nothing at all like the ones she would have worn three months ago either, those shabby country garments that spoke of a life tempered by ill health and routine long gone, and the highly coloured velvets she had replaced them with as unusual as they were practical.

Unconventional.

Original.

Incomparable.

Words that were increasingly being used to describe her in the local papers and broadsheets.

She liked the sound of them, the very choice such description engendered. No expectation or cloying pragmatic sensibleness that had been the hallmark of her years with Frankwell.

She did not think of him now as the man who had hurt her, the image of an angry bully replaced by the child who had lingered longer. Hopeful and dependent.

When he had died she had laid him in his coffin with an armful of Michaelmas daisies because they had been his favourite and the church had rung with the sounds of children's songs, the same tunes that he himself had sung in his final moments of life on this earth.

Sorrow had been leached though here in London, her life filling with new friends and new experiences. How fortunate she had been to have the Hardy sisters as neighbours, for within a week of arriving here their wide group of acquaintances had become her friends as well, their social standing making her own acceptance into society seamless. When they had taken her under their wing and encouraged her dream of having such a forum in her own salon she could barely believe the speed with which the whole idea had taken shape. Sometimes when she looked in the mirror and saw the way she smiled she could not remember the sombre woman who had fled Ipswich in a snowstorm.

Breathing out, she tried to stop the name that would come to her mind next. No, she would not think of him, of that night, of the way that he had left without even once glancing back; when her friend Elspeth Hardy came into the room with another pile of papers in her hands, Bea was glad of the interruption.

'We have nowhere at all to put those, Elspeth. Perhaps if you could take them back upstairs we may discuss the contents next week.'

'But they talk of the habit of wife selling, a topic that has been raised before—I wondered if they might add to the discussion?'

Bea screwed up her nose. 'I have read many accounts of such a practice, and have become increasingly of the view that the intention of these bargains is a way in which a woman can move on with her life, both parties having agreed to the proceedings.'

'You are not against them? I cannot believe it of you!'

Beatrice laughed. 'Often the purchaser is a lover. Would you not countenance such a path, given the impossibly difficult and expensive alternative of filing for a separation through church or court?'

'I do not know. Perhaps you might be right…'

'We will think about it later, for tonight I have prepared a talk on the ills of piracy and the human cost to such a vocation.'

'Piracy! A topic that should appeal to the growing number of men now attending! Have you not noticed that, Bea? Over the last month we have had an almost equal composition of the sexes, which is…encouraging to say the least.'

Beatrice nodded and sought out the trays to set. The new financial independence that she had inherited on the death of her husband was sometimes bemusing and she still liked to do as much around the home as she had when her situation had been less flush.

Tonight, though, she felt nervous for some reason, her heartbeat heightened and her hands clumsy. When she dropped a cup it shattered on the parquet floor and as she bent to pick up the shards of china one cut deep into her forefinger.

The blood welled immediately, running down her palm and threatening the sleeve of her gown. Snatching at the muslin cover used for the cakes, she was thrown back into that darkened carriage outside Maldon when Taris Wellingham had offered her the square of material wrapped around the fruitcake as a scarf. At the time she had barely thought about it…but now? Other things began to pile into recollection. The way he used his hands and the scar that marred his forehead. No small accident that. An injury collected when he was a soldier, perhaps, or a little later…

'Shall I find a bandage, Bea, or is that stopping?' Elspeth's sister Molly had come to join them.

'No, it is all right, thank you.' She gingerly took the fabric away and was relieved when the skin looked knitted and clean. The fear in her very bones did not diminish, however, and when the clock in the hallway struck seven o'clock she jumped visibly. Two days ago, as she had walked along the street to the bank, a man had jostled her quite forcibly, the pile of papers she held in her hands scattering around her. He had stayed long enough to peruse the contents and then had disappeared, neither helping her nor apologising.

He had seemed angry, though she could not truly catch sight of his face to determine if she had met him before. Perhaps the outwardly Bohemian nature of her lifestyle had galvanised him into a reaction that was rooted in fear. Fear that, should women start to think, they might displace men who were less astute in the work-force and in society. Her roots in business probably added to the equation, as the Bassingstoke fortune had been wrought from the hard sweat of rolling iron for the ever-burgeoning railway.

The whole thing was probably harmless, but added to the accident in the coach she was beginning to feel… watched.

Beatrice shook her head hard. It was half an hour before the first men and women would be arriving and she still had much to do. All this ruminating on a perceived menace would neither get the room organised nor help her ridiculous case of the jitters. Smiling at Elspeth and Molly, she resolved to put her worries aside, and, plumping the cushions in the room, she dusted off the seats of the chairs and sofas.

The downstairs salon was full to bursting and the discussions were under way when a new arrival made

Beatrice stop in mid-sentence, for the woman who had run into the open arms of Taris Wellingham in the barn was here.

Emerald Wellingham?

A wave of embarrassment washed away any sense of the argument she was trying to forward. Why would she come? What possible reason would bring her here, for surely she had understood her brother-in-law's wish for distance as he had left the barn so quickly after the carriage accident? The Duchess of Carisbrook was a beautiful woman, her countenance in this room even more arresting, if that was at all possible, than it had been in a snow-filled night.

'As I was saying…' Bea could barely remember the thread of her prose. Would the woman tell others here of her escapade, bringing up the scandal of her night alone in the company of an unmarried man for all to judge? Lord, if any of it should be known, her presence would hardly be countenanced in polite company, an ageing widow who had crossed a boundary that brooked no return.

Ruin!

And that was only with the knowledge of half of it. Taris Wellingham's hands in places no one had ever touched before, the waves of pure delight that had run across her body, melding it into rapture.

Tearing herself back to the topic under discussion, she finished off her speech. '…and so I reiterate again that many of these so-called pirates were refugees from the gaols of the world or deserters from the rigours of harsh naval discipline.'

'So you do not think some were just natural-born leaders who chose a life of crime by instinct, piracy being an attractive proposition when measured against what might have otherwise been available to them at home?'

Emerald Wellingham asked the question of her and there was a burst of discussion around the room as Bea tried to answer it.

'There are some who would agree with you. Some who might even say that piracy was an honourable, if not a noble, profession.'

A man interjected. 'These people were murderers who committed untold acts of barbarity on the open seas. They are not to be excused.'

'Priests and magistrates and merchants in the West Indies excused them all the time, sir. Money sometimes has a louder voice than morality.'

Emerald Wellingham again! Beatrice felt swayed by her argument.

'Indeed.' She sought for the words that might not alienate a group of folk who were by and large titled and wealthy. 'If one was from the West Indies, the availability of goods sacked by the pirates might have been considered a godsend.'

'You speak of heresy.' The same man as before spoke and his face had reddened.

'And of conjecture,' Beatrice added with a smile. 'For such stories are often that of fable and myth and it could take one a lifetime to truly know the extent in which they were entangled.'

She hoped such a platitude might console the man's anger and was relieved when it seemed to, and Elspeth's announcement of a light supper was timed well.

As all those present moved through into the dining room, Beatrice tidied her notes and when she looked up, Emerald Wellington stood beside her.

'For a woman of strong views you are remarkably diplomatic.'

'Perhaps because a heart attack of a patron at one of my soirées may not be conducive to their continuation.'

'And it is important to you that they do…continue?' Emerald's green eyes slanted bright against the lamp-light. Was this a threat? Had she come for a reason? Laughter surprised Bea.

'You remind me of myself, Mrs Bassingstoke. Myself a few years ago when the past held me immobile.'

'I do not know what it is you speak of. Now if you will excuse me…'

'My brother-in-law mentions you often. I think it was your bravery that impressed him the most.'

Anger made Bea feel slightly faint. Certainly his in-spiration was not gained from her beauty or her easy giving of love.

'I wondered if you would perhaps come and take tea with me. Tomorrow at half past two.' Emerald Wellingham placed her card on the top of the papers and waited.

'Thank you.' Beatrice had no possible reason to be rude and she had always prided herself on her good manners.

'Then you will come?'

For a moment the hard edges in her green eyes slipped and supplication was paramount. Still Bea could not quite say yes.

'It would just be the two of us…?' she began, for if it should be the whole of the Wellingham family she would not chance it.

'It would.' Quickly answered as though the Duchess had thought such a question might be voiced.

'Then I would like that.'

The other bowed her head. 'Until tomorrow, then.'

'You will not stay for supper?'

'I think not. My opinions on piracy could never meld with those of the others here and I would not wish to make a…nuisance of myself. However, I look forward to some privacy together.'

A small nod of her head and she was gone, the gown she wore bright against the more sombre shades of the others present and her gilded curls catching corn and gold and red.

A beautiful woman and a puzzle! Yet as Beatrice stacked the papers beneath her arms she had the strangest of feelings that they could one day be the very best of friends.

'I saw Beatrice-Maude Bassingstoke today, Ashe. She runs weekly discussions on current topics with the Hardy

sisters and is not a woman inclined to just parrot the opinions of the day.'

'What sort of a woman is she, then?' Her husband's
fingers traced a line down her arm, as he pulled off his
clothes and joined her in bed.

'An interesting one. I can well see why Taris was rather
taken by her. She is unexpectedly…fascinating.'

'High praise coming from a woman who seldom enjoys
"society".'

Laughing, Emerald wound her fingers through his. 'Has
your brother said anything else about that night to you?
It's just that I do not think it was quite as innocent as he
might insist it was.'

'I doubt Taris would be pleased to have you question
him, Emmie. Certainly he has shied well away from the
topic with me.'

'Mrs Bassingstoke blushed bright red when I mentioned
your brother and this from a woman who had just stood in
front of a roomful of strangers espousing theories that
excused those guilty of piracy as needy and forgotten
members of the communities they had been hounded out
of.'

'A fairly radical point of view, then.'

'Exactly!'

'Every woman Taris meets finds him attractive. Perhaps
your answer lies in that.'

'And they last but a moment when he realises that
beauty is so…transient and he is too clever to be long
amused with a siren who has little to say.'

'You speak as though the combination of beauty and brains is impossible, yet I have achieved it in you.'

She threw the pillow behind her at him and he caught it, a look in his eyes that told her discussing anything would soon come to an end.

'Beatrice-Maude Bassingstoke has a quiet comeliness that is apparent when you talk to her. She is possibly the cleverest woman I have ever had the pleasure to en-counter, but there is also something hidden about her...'

'Which you should well recognize, given all the secrets you kept buried from me.'

'I invited her here tomorrow, for afternoon tea.'

'God!' He sat up. 'Taris will be back from Beaconsmeade about then!'

Emerald merely smiled.

'If this backfires on you, I won't be pulled into being the cavalry...' Tweaking a long golden curl, he pulled her down across him. 'But enough of subterfuge. Show me lust and passion, my beautiful pirate.'

When she started to laugh he simply removed the sheet and placed his hand in a place that took away mirth.

'Love me, Emerald,' he whispered.

'I do.' Two little words that fell into the heart of every-thing!

Chapter Five

Taris arrived back in London in the early afternoon and he was worried. A report on the carriage accident had come to him a few weeks back and it was not as simple as he may have thought it.

The axle had been cut, sawed through to within an inch of the circumference, the shearing off of the wheel a deliberate and callous action from someone who wanted to create mayhem. Well, he had. One man was dead and the driver's fingers would never be right again, banishing the man and his family to penury for the rest of his life.

Well, not quite, his thoughts so akin to high drama that they made him smile. He had offered the man both a job and a cottage at Beaconsmeade, the substantial property he had inherited from his uncle three years ago.

Who the hell did the person responsible want to harm? Was it him? He sifted through memory. In his life there had been many things he had done that might invite such an action. Yet why now and why there in the middle of a county he seldom visited? Who else, then, could have been the target? Not the innocuous and timid mother and son, he decided, or the sensible and level-headed Mrs Bassingstoke. Perhaps the perpetrator had achieved his goal, then, with the demise of the snoring gentleman? He ran his fingers across his eyes and felt the beginning of an ache that was familiar around his left temple.

He tried not to remember that night in the snow, tried not to wonder what had happened to Beatrice-Maude. It was better she slipped into the delight of memory, a favoured recollection when everything else had faded.

Lord. He had not had a woman apart from her in over two years, the sheer difficulty of arranging it all and appearing 'sighted' too impossible to contemplate. Easier to lie in bed and just remember, he decided, for the number of people who actually knew his vision to be so poor could still be counted upon one hand.

Asher. Emerald. Lucy, Jack and Bates. A profound sense of shame and inadequacy rubbed up against anger. Five people were all that he wanted knowing of it too. Just them. He did not wish to walk into a room and feel that others judged him on what he could not see. He had always been a physical person, a fine shot, a good horseman, a man who had used his world from one wide edge of it to the other.

To be reduced to dependence and vulnerability would be... He could not even find a word for what he thought, could not dredge from the sheer and utter terror of his situation a phrase to encapsulate the horror.

He tried to keep his forays into society at a minimum

and he hated the busy rush of cities. Tomorrow, however, he had an appointment with his lawyer and needed to be there early. He preferred Beaconsmeade and the rolling greenness of the Kentish countryside, places he could walk and work and where the air smelt clean and breathable and infinitely less defiled.

Listening to the horses' hooves on the first paved stones of the town, he counted the corners.

Fifteen.

The Carisbrook town house should almost be in sight now. Securing his cane, he prepared for the carriage to stop. Bates at his side was doing the same.

'You have no plans at all for this evening, sir. I did not accept the Claridges' invite as you instructed me to, though your brother wrote to inquire whether you would be there.'

'He is almost as reclusive as I am and he only wants to know of my absence to make sure of his own.'

'There is, however, a ball at the Rutledge mansion tomorrow evening at which you are expected to appear.'

Taris frowned, trying to understand why his presence should be in any way necessary.

'The Earl of Rutledge is a supporter of the Old Soldiers' Fund, a charity of which you are the principal patron, sir. I did remind you last week of the affair.'

'I see. Could I not just pledge a great deal of money—?'

'The Duke of Carisbrook put your name forward to speak, sir.'

Damn, Taris thought. Asher and his efforts to get him

out and about! Sometimes he could happily strangle his brother for his meddling, born out of guilt.

'Very well, then.' Acquiescence was easier than the alternative of making a fuss and he made himself dwell on other things. It would be good to see Ruby, Ashton and Ianthe, for it had been all of a month since he had seen his nieces and nephew. He hoped Emerald's man Azziz would also be down from Falder, for he enjoyed a game of chess.

Family. How it wound around isolation with determination and resilience, the irritations of prying a small price to pay for all that was offered.

As the horses prepared to stop he readied himself to alight. There were many things he could still do and the familiarity of the town house made it possible for him to enter it without assistance.

Morton, the family butler, was the first to greet him, taking his hat and cloak at the door.

'Welcome back, my lord. We heard that the weather in the south has been kind the past month.'

'Indeed it has, Morton. Perhaps I might persuade you to have a sojourn at Beaconsmeade…'

The servant laughed. This discussion was one they had had for years, the head butler not a man with any love for country air.

The sound of voices from the downstairs salon stopped him in his tracks, and as he made his way from the lobby he tilted his head. Not just any voice! He felt the tension in him fist, hard-stroked against disbelief.

Mrs Beatrice-Maude Bassingstoke was here! Here. Ten

yards away, her honeyed husky voice with the slight soft lisp, speaking with his sister-in-law. His fingers tightened across his cane and he wished he had not left his hat with Morton. Concentrate, he admonished himself, as he counted the steps into the room.

Beatrice lifted the cup of tea to her lips and sipped, refusing the offer of sweet cakes from the maid as she did so.

Emerald Wellingham opposite her was charming, but there was an undercurrent of something she could not quite understand. A slight anxiety, if she had to name it, and a decided watchfulness.

'Your soirées are gaining the favour of all of society here in London. It seems that we have been bereft of fine debate in our town for far too long.'

'Debate or controversy, your Grace? There are some who might say such opinions serve to alienate reason.'

'But I am not one of them, Mrs Bassingstoke. And please do call me Emerald.'

Beatrice nodded. 'You have a beautiful name. My first name merely makes people grimace. Beatrice-Maude. The names of my two grandmothers lumped together, I am afraid, and hardly charming like your own.'

'Can they be shortened?'

This was the second Wellingham to ask her such a thing! She felt the sheer weight of it as an ache.

As in Bea-yond. As in Bea-utiful or Bea-witching! She had never said her name since without remembering…

'Bea?'

The voice from behind made her start. His voice. Here? The tea that she had been holding spilt down the front of her dark burgundy gown as she turned, feeling the Duchess's gaze on her own.

Taris Wellingham came forward with the movement of a man who had had too much to drink, catching the edge of the partly opened door with his shoulder and jerking back and around to lose his footing and fall heavily against the solid mahogany side cabinet. As he flailed to find a true direction his head tilted as if listening and his eyes looked strangely disorientated.

Swearing, he began to search the floor with his hands and Bea was instantly taken back to the days before her husband's turn. The days when Frankwell had imbibed too much whisky and had come home in exactly the same fashion.

Hollowness consumed her, and the impact of everything made her shake. The way he held himself against the line of the door to steady his balance, all expression on his face devoid of warmth even as he hoisted himself up, the beginning of a bruise that would show full dark upon his cheek on the morrow matching the tendrils of his hair loosened from the queue at his nape.

Years of living with a difficult man tumbled down on Beatrice-Maude in that one small isolated moment. Long years of anguish and guilt, her unpredictable sham of a marriage wrung into one dreadful feeling.

Panic!

To get away. To run from one who had caught at fancy and hope and imagination, yet was blighted with the same curse her husband had been dammed with.

She needed to escape, to be back again in the world of freedom and ideas that had just opened up to her, her autonomy and lack of restraint so far from the endless dread of hurt inflicted by a brandy-loosened temper.

'I must go.' Setting down her cup with a rattle, she hated the sound of alarm so easily heard in her voice.

'Perhaps you do not remember my brother-in-law…'

'Of course I do.'

Pushing past them both, Beatrice-Maude did not stop even to retrieve her cloak from the astonished servant at the front door. Outside she took a breath of cold air and simply ran, for the corner, for her home, for the safety of her rooms away from anyone, the hat in her hands unfastened and the gloves in her pocket unworn.

'Well,' Taris said as the silence inside the town house lengthened, 'I presume that means she does not favour the nickname Bea.'

Emerald laughed, though there were tears in her voice when she replied, 'I thought she was a sensible woman. I thought that she had impeccable manners and for the life of me I cannot understand what just happened.'

'At a guess I would say she saw I lacked sight.'

Silence confirmed his suspicions. Emerald might be able to see what he could not, but he could hear what others never did.

Fear. Abhorrence. And the need for flight.

He made himself smile, made his face carefully bland, the anger that was building hidden behind indifference even as his left cheek throbbed.

'Mrs Bassingstoke did not know before?'

'It was night,' he returned.

'And you are good in the darkness!'

'Precisely.'

'So good that she could spend the whole time with you and never guess?'

'It seems that is true.'

'I think I hate her for this.' Her voice was small, the anger in it formidable. 'And everything that happened today is my fault. Ashe told me to leave it alone.'

'But you didn't?'

'And now you despise me.'

'Hardly.' His left hand went out to feel along the lintel of the door, the shadows in the room long with darkness. For the first time ever he felt…nearly blind, the infinite gloom pressing down almost as a living thing. Intense and pressured, the foreverness of it just around the corner.

Where was Beatrice-Maude Bassingstoke now? How had she got home? Was home far? Would she be safe? The faint smell of flowers lingered in the air beside him and he breathed in hard, trying to keep her close and angry that he should even think to do so.

Beatrice sat on the side of her bed and cried. She did not try to be quiet, she did not wipe her tears away with a dainty handkerchief. She did not care which servant might eavesdrop or which friend calling in the afternoon might overhear her howls of anguish.

She just cried. For everything that had happened. For her appalling manners and her incredible rudeness, for the lack of control in Taris Wellingham's movements and for the knowing look of complicity on his sister-in-law's face.

The man she had admired was a drunkard!

Everything that had held her up in the past months was lost. Her confidence. Her belief in herself. Instead she was tossed back to the time when she had been completely at the mercy of the moods of a man whose anger or temperance depended on the amount and strength of the drop he had imbibed.

A few beers and he would drag her to his room. A few more and he would hit her. And a few more than that...

Never again. Never, never again!

Using the sleeves of her gown to wipe both her nose and her cheeks, the quick swipes threw her back to Ipswich and the house there.

Frankwell had been a big man and a bully, though after his apoplexy he had become kinder, his mind not quite remembering who it was she had been.

His wife. The positions changed over only a matter of weeks and the man with no family at all save her was as dependent as a three-year-old. There was no choice in any of it. There was no help to garner, with his finances tied to a lawyer who was living well on the interest of the

Bassingstoke money just as long as the main recipient of it was alive.

And the last years had slipped by with all the hardship of twice their number, the factories belching out high-grade iron even with an absentee owner at their helm.

Her life became days and weeks and months disappearing into the drudge of looking after a husband she had hated. Suddenly Beatrice was overcome with everything. With the past and the present and the future and she could not breathe, could not take the proper amount of air without the stinging contracting ache in the back of her throat stopping everything.

'Mama,' she whispered and thought of her parents, dead by the time she had reached the tender age of seventeen and thankfully unaware of the type of man that they had chosen for her husband.

The joy of the night in the snow came unbidden, taunting and mocking against the reality of what had happened today.

Today she had understood that the fatuous dreams of an ageing widow were destined to remain ever that, her life divided into before and after one perfect night.

Because now she knew and that was the very worst of it! Now she had had a taste of what it was to be delighted and pleasured and cared for, the impossible hope sending her into new fits of sobbing.

A knock on the door made her stop, as she pressed her lips together and frantically rubbed at her eyes.

'Yes. Who is it?'

'It's Sarah, madam. Might I come in?'

Looking at her face in the mirror as she stood to open the door, Beatrice grimaced, her eyes swollen and her cheeks blushed.

Sarah, her maid, stood at the door with a worried expression. 'Cook says that we will be having chicken tonight and he will prepare it in just the way you like it.'

'That will be lovely. Thank you, Sarah.'

'If there is anything any of us could do to help, ma'am...'

'I would certainly tell you if there was. Thank you again.'

Shutting the door, Bea felt like a woman who had let everybody down. She had had many servants before, of course, but never ones that had become her friends as these ones had.

Still, today she could not find it in herself to speak of anything, her disappointment in the character of Taris Wellingham such a calamity that she could barely believe it.

Was his over-drinking something that was known in society? It was only mid-afternoon and very early to be so befuddled and yet she had never heard even a whisper of it.

She breathed out and crossed to the window. The park opposite was filled with people, laughing happy people. People with lives that were so different from her own! Placing her palm on the glass, she enjoyed the momentary impression of cold and the frosted outline left when she removed it. Still here! Still attracted to men who could bring her nothing save heartache.

'Taris.' She whispered his name into the dusk. Strange that she had not smelt the liquor upon him as he had entered the room, which was something she had become adept at doing when Frankwell had returned home after a night out. No, all she had smelt was the tang of masculinity with an underlying hint of an astringent soap.

She wished she had not accepted Emerald Wellingham's offer of afternoon tea because then she might have never known…

'Stupid,' she chided herself, and, tying back her hair, decided to spend the rest of the evening cataloguing her new books.

She saw Taris Wellingham again in the Book Society Library the very next afternoon, perusing the shelves with another man she did not recognise.

Today his clothes were immaculate and worn in the fashion of one who did not place too much importance on the way a cravat was tied or any other such frippery. The bruise on his cheekbone, however, had darkened and swollen.

It was too late for her to stand and make her way out as he was only a few feet away and coming closer. Consequently she merely sat, pasting what she hoped was an expression on her face that would relate the disappointment she felt in what had happened yesterday.

He passed her by without acknowledgement, and so

close that she could hear what it was they were talking about.

Fox hunting and the hounds used at a 'meet'.

The cut direct! She grimaced. In all honesty there were many after all who might consider the inability to stop heavy drinking as a small thing, and others who might laugh at the notion of a man who would lose himself in the unmindful disregard of drink. But these people could not have lived with someone whose very personality was being eaten away by it, exposing layers beneath that were hardly humorous.

As she had! She decided that to say nothing would be an act of cowardice on her behalf.

'Excuse me, Lord Wellingham?'

He turned immediately and waited, as did the man with him. 'Mrs Bassingstoke.'

'I wondered if I might have a moment alone with you, sir?'

'Jack.' Said with all the authority of a dismissal to the man next to him. Beatrice remained silent until the other was out of hearing range.

'I would like to apologise for my behaviour yesterday, my lord. I realise that it was most unacceptable to leave a room in such a fashion, but in my own defence I might say that I have had some unfortunate experiences in my life because of heavy drinking.'

A heavy frown marred his forehead. 'I was not—?'

She didn't let him finish. 'Denial is one of the first signs that something is amiss, as I am sure you must be aware.'

'You think I cannot manage my drink?'

'The poor effect it has on your balance is certainly a telling symptom especially so very early in the day.'

A smile began to play around his lips and Bea hated the answering heavy thud of her heartbeat when she saw it.

'The good news is that there are remedies one might attempt.' Today he barely looked at her, glancing over her head as though something was far more interesting across the room, though his next question was heartening.

'What is it then that you would suggest?'

'Some would say exercise to be the most beneficial.'

'To keep my mind off the thought of another brandy?'

'Exactly.' She did not understand the humour that accompanied his question. 'The most important thing, however, is to admit that you do have a problem; if one holds the notion that this affliction is trifling...'

'I can assure you, Mrs Bassingstoke, that I do not think my affliction trifling.'

For the first time since she had begun talking to him she felt that they had the same viewpoint. 'Your measure of honesty is something that should help then, my lord.'

When he remained silent she took her courage in hand. 'Have you spoken to your family about this?'

'As little as I possibly can.'

'Would it help to speak to me of it?'

The silence was deafening.

'I am a woman who would respect every confidence.'

'I know you to be that.'

When his smile took on a quality of wickedness she realised exactly what he had said and flushed a bright beetroot red. 'I did not mean, of course, to allude to the night we spent—' She stopped as another thought struck her. Perhaps he had not meant that at all. She was too far in, however, to just pull back now. 'I would never say anything of it—we had both agreed that we should not.'

As she moved to one side he did the same and their hands touched. She felt her heartbeat quicken, to know again that living spark of recognition.

Jerking away, she looked around to see if anyone watched them and was horrified to notice patrons hurriedly averting their eyes. Taris Wellingham was a man who drew the notice of all those around him, with his height and his presence and his bearing. He was a man who looked as though he did not fit into the dusty quietness of this reading room, but should be on a battlefield somewhere, danger imprinted in his eyes.

'When could we start?' His question in the light of such thoughts disorientated her.

'Pardon?'

'When is it that you would begin helping me?'

'You are saying that you would like me to try?'

'Indeed. After such an eloquent persuasion why should I not?'

'Some men may be…too timid to admit to such a fault.'

'Not me.'

'Then you are unusual in such honesty, my lord, and I admire you all the more for it.'

His lopsided frown concerned her.

'If you are free tomorrow, perhaps a walk in the park might be a good beginning.'

'I am sometimes a little uncertain of my footing in wide-open spaces. The vestiges, I suppose, of the drink wearing down my balance.'

'Then I shall, of course, help you.'

'How would you do that?'

'Would it be frowned upon if I threaded my arm through your own, my lord?'

He shook his head firmly.

'Perfect,' she answered, feeling for the first time in two days a little more in control of everything. She had let Frankwell get worse and worse without doing anything. Could his own redemption have been as easy as Taris Wellingham's? My God. Why had she not tried such a remedy for him?

She knew the answer even as she asked the question. Because she had hated him, hated her husband and everything he stood for and in the late-night drunken ramblings he took by the river she always hoped he might just trip and sink unbeknown into the murky depths of the water. Guilt rose in force, as did contrition, though when the companion she had first seen with Taris Wellingham reappeared in the background she could tell that he was waiting for them to finish.

'I do hope to hear from you, my lord, regarding a time and a place for this exercise.'

'Oh, you will, Mrs Bassingstoke.'

'And I shall not say a word about anything we have discussed today…'

'A sensitivity that I should ever be grateful for.'

'There is one other thing that I would suggest, if I may.'

'Yes?'

'Throw out all the strong liquor in your house and replace it with water. That way temptation is never close at hand.'

His laugh reverberated around the space they stood in as she gave him her goodbye and hurried for the door.

Temptation?

Lord, it was not the drink he was tempted by, but the sound of her voice and the feel of her skin against his when he had moved and touched her by mistake.

Too damn tempted! He forced down desire as Jack Henshaw spoke.

'Who is she?'

'Mrs Beatrice-Maude Bassingstoke from Ipswich. She was one of the occupants of the carriage accident I was involved in.'

'She had much to say to you?'

'She thinks I am a drunk.'

'Why the hell would she think that?'

'Because the other day she saw me lose my footing and my direction. I would guess from what she does not say that her husband used to be a heavy drinker and, putting two and two together, she has come up with five.'

'You didn't enlighten her then, I gather?'

'You know me too well,' he drawled back. 'Blindness or a predilection for the bottle? Which one would you pick?'

Jack stopped walking. 'It's got a lot worse, then? Your eyesight?'

Taris nodded and made to walk on, irritated when Jack stayed firm.

'There are doctors who might help you if you went to see them.'

'Which I won't be doing.' Lord, he had done the rounds of the medical fraternity when he had first returned home from Jamaica and not one of them had been hopeful; his denial at what they had told him curled up into a harder anger. He did not wish to be hauled off again to a physician who would only disappoint him and the risk of gossip emanating from such a visit was too high. No. He would fight this creeping blindness on his own terms and in his own way. He swore it.

Another thought surfaced. What would happen should Beatrice determine the truth? Today with the full light of the window upon her he had made out the outline of her face. Not in detail, but not in grey sludge either. A halfway point to knowing what she might look like. He wished he could have used his fingers to fill in the nuances and touch her. Again. Even though he knew the foolhardiness of doing just that.

Taris Wellingham and his carriage arrived at her door almost exactly at two, after sending a note earlier to ask whether this time would be suitable.

Dressed in her bonnet, coat and gloves, Bea found him standing outside next to his coach. Today he wore brown, the colour showing up the darkness of his hair. Surprisingly he also wore a patch of the finest leather across his left eye.

'My lord,' she began, hating the tremor in her voice, 'have you been hurt?'

'No.' He did not elaborate or embellish his reply as he held open the door to a carriage emblazoned with a family crest and pulled by four perfect chestnut horses. Two footmen tipped their hats to her when she acknowledged them, both adorned in the livery of gold and blue.

Taris Wellingham followed her in, sitting in the seat opposite hers. Taking a breath, she smiled and tried to initiate some conversation between them.

'It is a beautiful day for this time of the year, is it not?'

'It is.'

'I have heard it said that such weather augurs well for the summer season. Some say that we should expect a very mild May.'

'A happy thought,' he returned in a voice that suggested anything but. 'And I would prefer it if you would call me Taris. With our history…' He stopped.

Our history? The weight of what had been between them settled like a stone in her stomach and the swelling bruise on his cheek underlined everything about him that was dangerous.

Today the ease of yesterday had gone, replaced by a tension that Beatrice could not understand as he watched her with a disconcerting directness, a small tic on the smooth skin below his one uncovered eye.

* * *

Hell! Taris thought. His eye was smarting and the headache that had been threatening all morning bloomed into pain. A familiar headache, the little sight that was left to him disappearing into nothingness. He should never have come, should have noted the heaviness in his temples and the tiredness in his eyes and cried off. But he was here and Beatrice-Maude was opposite with her quick-witted brain that might expose him as the cripple he was should he make even one false step. His fingers tightened on his cane, the silver ball his only connection to the world, his only certainty. All about him now lay the creeping dark of chaos and a discomfort that made him feel sick.

He had given his men instructions to stop at St James's Park, a place he often walked alone, because with the fences along the pathways on the western side he had a touchstone to know exactly where he was.

'I have been thinking up ways to try to help you with your…problem and was wondering if you would be averse to answering a few questions?'

She waited for his answer and he nodded.

'Do you drink often?'

'No.'

'But when you do drink, you drink a lot?'

The lies that were piling one on the other were nowhere near as humorous as he had found them yesterday.

I am almost blind and that is why I fell.

He should say it, just spit it out here and now and then

that would be the end of it, for the truth would send any woman fleeing.

But he did not say that because, even nauseous and in pain, the words just would not come.

Avoided. Adrift. Lessened.

Turning his face to the window, he pretended to look out, forcing away all the righteous arguments that rang in his head whilst protecting himself instinctively from pity.

As the conversation between them again spluttered to a halt, Beatrice tucked her hands into the dark red fabric of her new dress and stayed silent.

He did not want to speak, perhaps? He had asked her for this walk and now he regretted it? Her intent to help had become intrusive and he wished he might have never given her the chance to take the experiment further?

She hardly knew him, hardly understood a thing about him; this morning, with the patch across his eye, he looked not only wildly handsome, but also unbearably distant.

A lord and a man who walked his world in the very highest echelons of society and one who could hardly be relishing her busy-bodying ways and her plain, plain looks.

Her strident lecture on the ills of strong drink suddenly looked inadvisable and naïve. What did she truly know of him, after all, that a whore in one of the establishments off Covent Garden might not? An affair of the flesh and nothing of the heart.

'If you would prefer to leave our outing to another day, my lord, I would quite understand.'

She did not dare to chance the use of his Christian name, even given his directive of a few moments prior.

As if he suddenly remembered she was there, he turned.

'No, I should like to walk.' Again he did not look directly at her, his face guarded today and distant.

'Your horses are beautiful. I saw you once in Regent Street tooling greys.'

'Greys?' He looked puzzled.

'With a woman. A young woman with light hair.'

'Lucy. My sister. She insisted that she learn the art of managing a team.'

Relief turned inside Bea. Not a paramour, then, but a sibling. 'Indeed, she did look competent.'

'Where were you?'

'Buying a hat, my lord, and in awe of such a display as everyone else on the street most surely was.'

'I am sorry I did not see you.'

She could not let him off the hook so easily. 'Even though your glance brushed directly across mine…?'

He leaned forwards at her reprimand, his movements strangely careful. No clumsiness in them or extra exertion.

'Were you married long, Beatrice-Maude?'

The question was so personal that Bea wondered if she should have made certain that Sarah, her maid, had accompanied her. She shook her head, knowing that Taris Wellingham could not be interested in another dalliance three long months after so decidedly ending the first one.

'I was, my lord.'

'And he drank?'

Hot shame filled her and confusion. 'Occasionally.'

Nightly. Daily. Every moment by the end of it.

'But you showed him the error of his ways and led him into abstinence?'

'No, my lord, God in his wisdom showed him that.'

A malady to take away any choice.

He nodded, but did not reply. The sweat that had built upon his forehead worried her, the sheen of it mirrored by the heavy lines on his forehead.

Pain!

He was in pain, she thought, and was doing his level best not to let her see it. His knuckles showed white where he clutched on to the silver ball of his cane and the scar that trailed from his hairline into the soft leather of his patch twitched. She wondered how he had received it. A bullet when he had served in the army? Or was it a duelling scar?

The shout of the footman stopped any further thoughts, however, and Beatrice saw that they were now at the park.

On alighting she noticed that the pathway in this particular section of the park was ringed with a fence, markings carved into the railings. Taris Wellingham's fingers ran across the nicks in the wood. He seldom wore gloves, she noted, as was more customary for gentlemen of the *ton*, and often ran his open palm along objects. As in the carriage outside Maldon when his touch had run along the line of her cheek. As in the barn where they had ventured further and she had turned into his loving…

* * *

Taris felt the directions carved into the railings, something he had had Bates take care of to ensure the continuation of a sense of independence that was being constantly threatened. He always used this place, always walked in exactly the same arc, down to the lake and then back again, the lack of any steps or rough areas a boon when he was alone. Or in company, he amended and smiled.

His headache was lessening in the fresh air, the tightness around his eyes dissipating. Even his sight seemed a little restored. He could now make out the row of trees at the end of the pathway and the rough shape of a bonnet that Beatrice wore. Not quite helpless, then. His black mood lightened.

'The smell of the trees in St James's reminds me of my home in Kent, which is why I come here.'

'You don't live in London?'

'I moved out three years ago when I inherited land.'

'Yet you choose to ride in a public conveyance?'

He nodded. How could he answer her? What could he say?

Sometimes I like to be by myself in the midst of people who know nothing about me, who would not care if I slipped or fell. People who might simply pick me up and go on their way, no labels attached because of the way our paths have crossed...

'I think I can understand the reason.' She was talking again, the lilt in her words attractive. 'I too gained a good living on my husband's death and old habits are hard to forget. Not that you would have old habits, of course, with your birth and name, but for me it was such.'

'Was he a good man...your husband? A man of honour?'

'I was sixteen years old when I married him and twenty-eight when he died. To admit failure over that many years...' Her voice petered out and he stepped in.

'So you admit to nothing?'

Her laughter was unexpected and freeing. A woman who would not take umbrage at even the most delicate of questions.

'I am now in a city that allows me the luxury of being whatever I want to be.'

'And that is?'

'Free.'

He remembered back to her questions on their night in the snowstorm and everything began to make more sense. Perhaps they were a pair in more ways than she had realised it? Two people trying to hew a future from the past and survive. Independently.

'But you still wear his ring.'

'Because I have chosen to accept what has been and move on.'

Such honesty made him turn away. Not so easy for him, as the scar across his temple burned with fear and loss. Not so easy for him when the darkness was there every morning when he awoke. Still, in such logic there was a gleam of something he detected that might save him.

Not acceptance, but something akin to it; for the first

time in three years Taris felt the anger that had dogged him shift and become lighter.

She had said something that unsettled him, and wished she might have taken back her words to replace them with something gentler. But she couldn't and any time for regrets was long past. Here with the wind in her hair she felt a sort of excitement that challenged restraint and allowed a wilder emotion to rule.

Her whole life had been lived carefully and judiciously. Today she felt neither, the feeling directly related to the man who walked beside her.

Walked fast too, his frame suggesting a man who was seldom indolent and her scheme of exercise in the light of that looked…questionable.

'I think perhaps you have not been quite honest with me, sir,' she began and he turned quickly, guilt seen and then gone, the intensity of it leaving her to wonder what he thought she might say. 'At a guess I would say that you are far more industrious in the art of exertion than I have given you credit for.'

'Honesty has its drawbacks,' he returned. 'With it, for example, I would not be enjoying this walk in the park.'

'You think I might pass you off as one who has no hope of resurrection?' She began to laugh. 'You do not strike me as a man who would have any need at all to lose himself in drink, my lord.'

'You might be surprised at the demons that sit on my shoulders, Mrs Bassingstoke.'

'Name one.'

'Your inability to treat me with the reverence I deserve.'

She laughed again. 'A paltry excuse, that. And if you do not have another better reason for taking to the bottle then I might abandon you altogether!'

'Would an inability to see anything properly at all be enough of an exoneration?'

Bea turned towards him. The tone of his voice had changed, no longer as light as it had been or as nonchalant.

And then she suddenly knew!

The patch. The cane. His fall at his brother's and the scar that ran full across his left eye. Like skittles, the clues fell into place one by one by one. No kind way to say it. No preparation. No easy laughter or words to qualify exactly how much he could see. Only the amber in his one undamaged eye burning brittle golden bright! Challenging and defiant.

The wind off the lake blew cold between them, his cloak spreading in its grip and his hand on the fence with its notched wooden carvings. Sight through touch. In that one second everything Bea had ever wondered about made a perfect and dreadful sense.

Blind?

'So you do not have a problem with drinking?' Her voice was quiet, laced with a truth that had not quite yet settled.

He shook his head. 'I do not.'

'Yet I have never heard anyone mention—'

'Because I have never told,' he shot back, defence in his posture and tight protection in the lines of his face.

'Anyone?'

'Asher, Emerald, Lucy, Jack Henshaw and Bates,' he murmured, the list as short as five.

Six now with her. Nobody really, for such a secret. 'And that is why you fell?'

He nodded. 'When you suggested a fondness of the bottle, it was easier than this.' His free hand gestured to his face, the silver-topped cane swinging in an arc as he did so, his anchor in a world of darkness.

Need. His need. Sliding in unbidden. Need of help and succour and support. She could not help the dread that crept into her voice, a thousand days of care for her husband reflected in such an unexpected truth.

'I promise you that I will be sworn to silence on this news, my lord,' she began, hating the withdrawal she could see, his head tilted against the wind as though listening to all that was further away. 'I would give you my word.'

'And I would thank you for it.'

Honourable even in hurt, fatigue written plainly on his face.

She no longer knew how to respond.

Blind! Such a small word for everything that it implied. Dependent. Reliant. Like Frankwell had been?

'Perhaps we should walk back to the coach. It is getting late and cold…'

His suggestion was formal and polite, the choice of

escape given under the illusion of time and weather. He did not wait for any answer, but surged ahead, his lack of sight pulling at her as he made his way up the path using the rail to guide him and his stick to monitor the lay of the ground.

The patch across his left eye was a banner of the shame that she felt when she failed to call him back to say that it did not matter, that it made no difference, and for the second time in two days a man, who had never been exactly as he seemed, threw her equilibrium into chaos.

Taris felt the ache around his temple tighten, constricting the blood that flowed into his last fading sight and band around a building pain.

God. What had made him tell her? What mistaken and stupid idea had crept into his head and made him blurt it out?

Take it back…take it back…take it back…

The voice of his anger was thickly strangled, bewildered by his admission and lost in fatigue.

All he wanted was to be home, away from her promises and the whisper of pity in her reply, the shocked honesty in her words underlain by another truth.

'I promise you that I will be sworn to silence on this news, my lord.'

Sworn to the silence of one who would distance herself from needing to be beleaguered by it? Sworn to the silence of one who would make a hurried escape from his person and count herself lucky? That sort of silence? In Beatrice-Maude's restraint he had a sudden feeling of breakage.

Spirit. Heart. And pride.

Tell anyone and open yourself up to the shame. Tell anyone and hear the shallow offer of charity.

When his hand clasped the rail on the carriage steps he hauled himself in and laid his cane across his knee. A fragile barrier against all that he wasn't any more and would never be again.

A lessened man. A needy man. A man who could barely get to the front steps of his own house without help. His unwise confession burnt humiliation into his anger at everything.

Bea did not cry when she was finally home. Did not rant and rail as she had when she had thought an inability to limit strong drink was his only problem.

Today she merely sat on the window-seat with the rain on the glass behind blurring the vista and the small clock beating out the minutes and the hours of silence.

The same sound she had measured her life against for ever!

Reaching across to the table, she picked it up and threw it hard against the ground, the glass shattering as the workings inside disintegrated. Springs and metal and the face of numbers spinning around, time flown into chaos and the beginning of a quiet that she could finally think in!

Exhaling, she stood and crossed to the mantelpiece, extracting a card from a small china plate and holding it close.

The Rutledge Ball would begin at ten and Taris Wellingham was one of the patrons.

Her heart beat faster as she formulated a plan.

Chapter Six

Taris Wellingham stood with his brother and Lord Jack Henshaw at the top of the room. Tonight he was in black and was 'much dressed', the cut of his coat and trousers impeccable, his hair slicked back in a fashionable manner and his boots of the finest leather. But it was the glasses that he wore tonight which drew Beatrice's attention.

She took a breath, hating the fact that he was by far the most handsome man in the room and she was by far the least beautiful woman. Still, she was not one to do things by halves and, starting forwards, she hoped that he would at least hear her out.

The arrival of the Countess of Griffin's daughter, Lady Arabella Fisher, a woman of whom Beatrice-Maude had heard much, thwarted her intentions as she rushed through the burgeoning crowd to the side of Taris Wellingham. Her smile told Bea that she was more than enamoured by him, though his answering expression seemed tight.

Others joined them, laughing at the things he said, though Bea was too far away to make sense of any words.

What she did make sense of was the sheer and utter number of women in this room who threw him hooded glances before making their way to his side.

She swallowed. Those around him were the very pick of this Season's débutantes, the cream of a society priding itself on lineage and ancestry. She recognised the Wilford sisters and the Wellsworth heiress, along with Lady Arabella, and was about to withdraw when a voice beside her made her jump.

'I did not think of you as a coward, Mrs Bassingstoke.'

Emerald Wellingham stood beside her, blocking her retreat.

'It seems then that my rudeness at your house the other day is not my only failure, your Grace.'

'Ahh, so formal when I thought you might be a friend?'

Bea's heart raced at the tone in her voice. Satirical. Taunting. And she could well understand why. 'You have cause to chastise me.'

The laugh that followed set Beatrice's nerves on edge.

'I would say you might have to fight your way through the gathering crowd of adoring females if you wish to speak to Taris.'

'So I see.'

'And if I thought that was all that you saw, Mrs Bassingstoke, I might turn this minute from your company and hope that you might never darken my family's door again with your prejudices. But there is more to you, I think. More to the singular reaction of panic that I saw on your face when you comprehended the nature of my brother-in-law's shortfalls.'

A voice behind made both turn and the Duke of Carisbrook joined them. 'Mrs Bassingstoke.' Said with all the indifference of a man who could barely feign politeness.

'Your Grace.' Bea wished that she just might disappear into the polished floor beneath her feet. Her palms, where she held her hands like fists, were damp with nervousness, though she made herself smile.

'If you will excuse me…'

She turned and walked through the crowd, the music of Mozart softening the hard cracks of anger that she felt boiling up in herself.

'*Tell no one…*'

Her mantra for the past decade as life had flung crisis after crisis her way, the little difficulties escalating into bigger ones, and all eminently unrectifiable.

Loud giggles from the group at the top of the room pierced her bewilderment, and she could not think what exactly to do next, though a balcony provided a way out and she slipped on to it, wiping the tears she felt pooling in her eyes as she tried to take stock of the situation.

She was twenty-eight years old and any histrionics on her part would be reprehensible and overblown, an aged woman who should have been well past undisciplined and unbecoming emotion.

The sheer and utter hopelessness of it all left her

gasping and she placed her hands upon her chest, barely breathing, the silence of just standing there bringing a measure of control.

And then the door opened and Taris Wellingham came towards her, his hands around the silver ball on his ebony cane.

'My sister-in-law informed me that you wished to see me.'

He sounded nothing like the man who had walked with her earlier in the afternoon, but all imperious and lofty.

'I did, my lord. I came tonight to tell you that I do not quite know what came over me today and that I would like to thank you.' Her voice was pulled from embarrassment, barely audible.

'Thank me?' His words were brittle. Almost harsh.

'Thank you for entrusting me with your secret…' She faltered and as he turned away she tried anew. 'I would also like to say that your affliction of poor eyesight is infinitely more appealing to me than the other option of drunkenness.'

Unexpectedly he turned back and smiled, though as the silence lengthened between them she simply could not think of one other thing to say.

'My sister-in-law tells me you have discussions on "matters of importance" at your residence.' He looked exactly at her tonight, amber magnified through the thick spectacles.

'Put like that, it all seems rather absurd,' she returned.

'She tells me that you are a woman of strong opinion and that your eyes are green. Leaf green,' he amended when she did not say anything. 'She also tells me that you worry a lot.'

'She could see that?'

'In the line on your brow.'

'An unbecoming feature, then,' Beatrice said, all her hackles rising. What else had Emerald Wellingham related to him? 'I am a plain woman, my lord.'

'Plain is an adjective that has many different interpretations. A carp in a river can be plain to the eyes of one who does not fish, yet vibrant to an angler. A deer in the forest can look insignificant amidst a band of sun-speckled trees and magnificent away from them. Which plain are you?'

'The type that recognises the truth despite any amount of flowery rhetoric.'

He laughed.

'Describe yourself to me, then.'

She hesitated. 'You can see nothing at all?'

'With my glasses on I know that you are not a large woman. I know too that your hair is long and thick and that you have dimples in your cheeks.' He held out his hands. 'From touch,' he qualified. 'There is a lot to be learned in touch. On a good day I can see more.'

'I am five feet two inches tall and some may call me… thin.'

'Some?'

'My husband always did. He thought that if I ate more I should appeal to him better, but no matter how much I tried—' She stopped, horrified as to what she had just confided in him, when for all the years of her marriage she had told every other soul nothing.

'Pride can be a dangerous thing, Beatrice-Maude.'

She pretended not to understand what he meant. But she knew exactly the tack that he was following because pride was all that had ever stood between her and chaos. Pride kept her quiet and biddable, because the alternative of others knowing what she had suffered was just too humiliating.

Honesty fell between them like a stone in a still and deep pond, the ripples of meaning fanning outwards as the consequences became larger and larger. Withdrawal had its own set of repercussions, just as pretence did. Still, here on the balcony, with the distant strands of Mozart on the air, she was careful. A woman with the candour of her past licking at twenty-eight long years and a future before her that finally looked a little bright. She could allow no one to tarnish that. Not even Taris Wellingham, with his magical hands and his handsome face.

No, plain was measured in more than just the look of one's countenance, she decided right then and there. Indeed, it was a bone-deep knowledge that no amount of clever repartee might disavow, a knowledge engraved with certainty in each memory and action and hope. Unchangeable, even with the very best of intentions.

When the door behind him opened to reveal Lord Henshaw, she used the moment to escape, excusing herself before walking away with the swift gait of one who was not quite breaking into a run.

Taris listened to her go, knew the exact moment that she disappeared from the balcony, her footsteps quick and urgent.

'You are due to speak in five minutes.'

'Rutledge sent you to find me?'

'He is a man who likes things to be on time.'

'May I ask you a question, Jack?'

'Go ahead.'

'What does Mrs Bassingstoke look like to you?'

'Mrs Bassingstoke?' Surprise lay in Jack's reply as Taris nodded. 'She is shapely in all the right places and her character is determined. If I were to pick just one word to describe her I would choose "original".'

'What colours does she favour in her clothes?'

'Bright ones.'

'And her hair? How does she wear that?'

'Pulled back, though errant curls show around her face.'

The silence between them was alive with questions. Then a burst of music alerted them to a change in the main salon and Taris felt Jack's arm against his own as they made their way inside.

Taris Wellingham's speech was received with all the acclaim that it deserved, Bea thought, as it came to an end, his articulate arguments as to the necessity of better treatment for those who had served in the army both persuasive and compelling.

'Lord Wellingham has a way with words,' she heard an older lady say behind her.

'And a way with the ladies! Look at how the young Lady Arabella Fisher is eyeing him up. There are whispers that the announcement of an engagement will be forth-coming and she is said to be extremely wilful.'

'Well, she certainly is beautiful and her father's land runs alongside Lord Wellingham's at Beaconsmeade.'

An engagement! Beatrice pushed her disappointment down as a waltz began and a flurry of excitement filled the room. She had no reason to hold any opinion on Taris Wellingham's love life. He was still young enough to take a bride and to all intents and purposes Lady Arabella Fisher was more than suitable. Pushing her fringe out of her eyes, Bea wished that she had been even half as beau-tiful, the thought so vain and vapid she almost laughed at it. What would happen when the woman found out that Taris's sight was not as it should be? Would she be kind?

Couples were now taking their places on the floor. Of all the dances this was the most intimate and the most favoured, the tedious figures of the quadrille something to be got through while one waited for the waltz.

Bea was just preparing to retire to the supper room, for she had seldom been asked to dance at any soirée, when a man appeared at her side.

'My master has sent me to ask you if you would accom-pany him in this dance.'

'Your master?'

The young man reddened.

'Oh, I am sorry. Lord Taris Wellingham is my master. He said that you know him.'

A quick spurt of shock kept Bea speechless, but she managed to nod and followed the Wellingham servant.

Taris stood alone by a pillar and seemed to know the exact moment she joined him, placing his arm forwards and tucking her hand in the crook of it when she laid it on his sleeve.

'I hope this means you have said yes to the dance, Mrs Bassingstoke?'

'You may not feel the same after I have trodden on your feet for a full five minutes or more, my lord.'

'You are telling me you are a poor dancer?'

'The very worst in the room, and one with a minimum of practice.'

'You do not enjoy dancing?'

'I did not say that, sir. It is just that I am seldom asked.'

'Then every man here must be blind.'

She could not help but laugh at his ridiculous comment, though when his arm came around her waist and his fingers clasped her hand she sobered. She had never danced this particular dance, not with anyone at all, though she had practised sometimes in the privacy of her room with a pillow.

Goodness, Taris Wellingham was hardly a pillow and they were so very close, her fingers entwined in his, her pliant body pressed against his hardness.

'You always smell the same.'

'The same?'

'Flowers. You use flowers as a perfume.'

'An attar of violets,' she returned, amazed that he had even noticed.

She felt him breathe in, tasting her, the sensual and tiny

movement poignant in the situation in which they now found themselves, and behind thick glasses his eyes were opaque amber and watching.

Would he like what he could still see? Did the plain he had spoken of look less inviting in the full light of the candles, a woman who only in fancy and hopefulness could ever stand a chance?

A chance of what?

Her thoughts turned in a tumble. She must not think like that! This was but a dance, a trifling thing and transitory. Around the perimeter of the floor she saw a hundred others watching them and was jolted back. Silly daydreams from a woman who after all wished for neither a permanent relationship nor marriage ever again and was hardly in a social stratum lofty enough to count as a would-be bride should she even want it.

'Are you in London for long, my lord?' She sought a neutral topic and the sensible tone in her voice was comforting.

'One week,' he answered. 'I rarely stay for any length of time.' As if he felt her withdrawal he loosened his hold and the gap between them widened. No longer pressed so close. No longer dancing as if they were the only couple on the floor.

'Perhaps, then, you might come to my discussion on Wednesday night.'

'Perhaps.'

She was not dissuaded by his tone. 'The topic is on the rights of a woman to her own property once she is married.'

He smiled. 'And you think that would hold my attention?'

'You are a well-educated man, my lord, and an articulate one. I would think that the unfairness of the situation, where by law virtually all of a woman's property becomes her husband's upon marriage, would be of interest to you.'

Again he smiled. 'You do not take into account my upbringing. As the sons of a duke, we were taught from the cradle that the notion of a husband being the guardian of his wife's land is just common sense.'

'Your own mother taught you that? Is she still alive?' Beatrice could not believe what she was hearing.

When his laughter rang across the room the other couples dancing close to them looked around.

'The change that you speak of does not happen overnight, Bea, and I should advise you to take care.'

'Take care?'

'Some members of the aristocracy may be averse to your liberal views.'

'The vested interest of men who would not benefit from change, you mean?'

'Exactly.'

'Are you one of those men?'

His fingers squeezed hers as if in warning. She noticed that he did not use much space on the floor. They had virtually danced in almost the same spot for the whole of the time.

'Sometimes opinions that are too strident can cause more trouble than they are worth. A wise woman would pick an argument she could win.'

She felt her heart beat faster and he must have felt it too for he tilted his head in the particular way he had of doing so.

'I would never hurt you, Beatrice. At least know that.'

'I do.'

Said with the conviction of a woman who did know, the strange intimacy between them confounding her with the very brevity of their acquaintance. She had never talked with anyone before as she had talked with Taris Wellingham, sparring with words and yet safe! Here was a man who was big enough to allow others their differing opinions whilst testing his own.

So unlike her husband!

'There is another matter that I should like to discuss with you,' he said. She felt him looking at her, felt the position of his body straight against her own. 'I have had a report on the cause of the accident. It seems that the wheel did not shear off on its own accord, but was assisted.'

'Assisted?'

'Sawn. Almost in half.'

Taris did not soften his words at all and when she tripped against him held her still.

'Someone tried to kill me?'

Her question was odd. 'There were five people in the carriage. What makes you think it was you that they were after?'

Her breath was taken in one trembling gasp and he knew even as she remained silent that there were things she had not told him, but the final strains of the dance had just ended and his brother moved over to join them.

'Thank you, my lord.' Beatrice was all distance and good manners and he tried to determine in which direction she had stepped away, but could not.

'I hope she gave you an apology for the other day.' Ashe placed his arm against his own.

'I think she gave me more than that.'

'The Bassingstoke money is forged in steel, Taris, Ipswich steel, and the workers as poorly paid and as underaged as any in England.'

'You have been busy, brother.' An edge of criticism curled in Taris's answer.

'I like to think of it as careful. The woman was with you overnight, after all, and I thought it only prudent to find out something about her.'

Hating himself for the question, Taris nevertheless asked it. 'And what did you find out about her?'

'She was widowed a month before the carriage accident, though few in the area knew her or her husband socially as they did not seem to mingle much. Indeed, it was said that she was rather reserved so I am hoping that she will not present...a problem.'

'Problem?'

'She is a widow of means. If she decided that your night together ruined her reputation, you might find yourself in trouble.'

'The woman came as a friend tonight, Ashe, not to hold me accountable for the consequences of a carriage accident.'

'Emerald implied that she could be interested in you in other ways.'

'Other ways?' Taris did not like the tone of entreaty in his query. What had Emerald seen that he himself had not? The feel of Bea against him was hard to forget. Even here in a roomful of women all vying for his attention he still sought the honeyed and gently lisping tones of the clever Widow Bassingstoke, yearning like an adolescent for her soft full breasts and for her eagerness.

'Emerald thought perhaps there was more to that night in the barn.'

'More?'

'Damn it, Taris, your name has been linked to no woman's since you returned from Jamaica and that does not come from any lack of interested women. My lady wife thought perhaps the…drought had been broken.'

'Drought? If you weren't my brother…'

'Then I wouldn't care at all,' Asher supplied before he could end the sentence. 'It is only because I am your brother that I take the time to try to protect you.'

'Well, don't, for I need neither a nursemaid nor a minder and if you feel I may sully the family name by dallying with someone unsuitable then perhaps you should look to your own recent past.'

'I didn't mean…if you liked her it would be different…'

'Enough, Asher. Rutledge would not take kindly, I think, to seeing two of his patrons having a fist-and-cuff in his salon and any association I choose to pursue with

Beatrice-Maude Bassingstoke is none of your damn business.'

'Very well. If you feel that strongly about her…'

Taris suddenly frowned, having the sneaking suspicion that he had just been taken for a ride in the dulcet tones of his sibling, and wondering too just what his defence of the Widow Bassingstoke actually meant.

He knew that she was still here, for he had caught the sound of her voice. His eyesight, however, allowed him no possible means of locating her again and he did not dare to chance sending Bates to wheedle the promise of another dance.

It simply was not done. One dance would not excite the comment two would, and already he could hear in the buzz of comments around him speculation about Beatrice-Maude and their possible relationship, as he seldom took to the floor at any of these soirées. He smiled. Seldom was probably putting a generous face on it—never would be the more appropriate term.

Chapter Seven

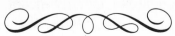

An assortment of calling cards and invitations arrived the next morning and Bea found them in a tidy pile on the salver on the hall table.

Lord, she thought as she sorted through them, the impressive list of names making her wonder. She remembered when Frankwell had received cards in Ipswich in the early years of their marriage and the lengths he had gone to arrange them where they might be the most visible.

For her part now she stacked them up and placed them face down, hoping that no one would make the effort to come and call and agitated by the fact that they might.

She knew exactly why she had suddenly become fashionable. It was the direct result of her dance last night with Taris Wellingham. She had heard it from her servants, who had heard it from those of the other grand houses, the grapevine of gossip as rapid and faultless as any paper in print.

Chewing on the edge of a nail, she glanced up and

caught sight of herself in the mirror above the mantel and was glad that Taris Wellingham could only see the vague outline of shapes.

If he could see properly, she doubted he would make the effort to dance with her at all. Perhaps everything she was imagining between them was pure falsehood.

She lifted her wrist to her nose and smelt. Violets. Her mother would pick posies sometimes and place them in her room in the old house above Norwich before she had been betrothed. Nearly half a lifetime ago.

When Elspeth appeared at the door a few moments later Beatrice was already sorting through a pile of new books in her library. This room of all the rooms in her house was the one she most favoured. To have a place where she could set out each tome was a delight above all the others and to read in the daylight without any inter-ruption was something she had not been able to do since…for ever.

'You look happy this morning, Bea. Could that have anything to do with your apparent success at the Rutledge Ball last night? Molly mentions the name of Lord Wellingham?'

'I danced only one turn with him, Elspeth,' she returned. 'In a ball with a programme of at least twenty-nine other dances I fail to see the significance of such an action.'

'Word is that he seldom favours the waltz. It also says that he has not danced at a soirée in years.'

Beatrice remained silent.

'Lord Taris Wellingham is one of the most powerful

men in England, Beatrice. He is the also the gentleman that all the young girls set their caps at and a lord who, although charming, is decidedly unavailable.'

Bea waited to see if Elspeth would mention the problem of his sight, but she did not. Still, as the silence lengthened she was loath to just leave it there.

'I heard some woman speak of a property… Beaconsmeade I think it was they said.'

'His seat in Kent. A magnificent house by all accounts it is too, and its master a man who should not be trifled with. You can see that in his visage, for the mark on his face is rumoured to have come from a pirate's bullet in the West Indies.'

'You are jesting with me, surely. What possible tie could the son of a duke have with such people?'

'I do not know. All I do know is that he is a man whom any woman, no matter what her age, might be swayed by.'

Bea began to laugh. 'The woman that you are alluding to meaning me?'

'Even a sensible woman has her dreams.'

'I was married for twelve years, Elspeth, and I can honestly say to you that the experience was such that I would never repeat it. Not for any man.'

'Oh, it was not marriage I was thinking of. I do not think he would offer that…'

A violent blush of red had Bea turning away. She felt her fingers shake as she reached for the collar of her dress, pulling the light wool from her throat to allow the slight feel of air against her skin.

His hand on her breast and his tongue tracing the shape of her nipple before pressing closer…

'Are you well, Beatrice? You seem somewhat distracted this morning.'

With an effort Bea pulled herself together.

'Your very liberal opinions are sometimes distracting—I was not born into a family such as your own with the penchant for expressing ideas that are…so radical.' When she saw the slight frown on her friend's face she hurried on to allay any worry. 'That is not a criticism of you, Elspeth, for I wish with all my heart that I could throw caution to the wind in the way that you so effortlessly seem to.' She was horrified as tears came behind her eyes, and the bone-deep desire in her breast for something more surfaced.

Taris Wellingham. He had sent no card this morning, just as he had not tried to approach her after the waltz they had shared. Perhaps his eyesight was such that he could not find her, though she suppressed that excuse; if the servant had sought her out before, then he certainly could do so again.

No! She tried to push the desire she felt for him beneath the easier banner of sense. Of course he would not be searching her out. She was a woman who had broken every rule of good sense after all. First with the easy giving of her body in the night-snowed barn and then again yesterday at the small park when she had failed to offer any support after his unexpected and genuine confession.

The heavy ring of her doorbell brought her from her reveries to find Elspeth had left. She listened to the sound of the visitor's voice with growing concern. A young woman's voice. But not one she recognized.

When the maid brought in her card, Bea was surprised. Lady Lucinda Wellingham! Bea indicated that she would receive her and sat down to wait, not wanting to appear quite as flustered as she felt upon hearing the name.

'Mrs Bassingstoke?' The same woman tooling the horses in Regent Street all those weeks ago came into her room. Not daintily either, but with a decided purpose. Bea noticed she did not wear gloves and that the hat she had donned barely covered her silky blonde hair.

Beautiful. Like all the Wellinghams were beautiful, though her fair hair and blue eyes were not mirrored in either of her brothers.

'You are Mrs Beatrice-Maude Bassingstoke, are you not?' she asked, a heavy frown easily seen between her brows.

'I am,' Bea returned and stood, though she was nowhere near as tall as this newcomer and wished suddenly that she had kept her seat.

'The same Mrs Bassingstoke involved in an accident with my brother Taris between Ipswich and London?'

'The very same.'

'Then I am pleased to meet you.' Her wide smile was both puzzling and welcome. 'Very pleased to meet you, in fact—I am Lady Lucinda Wellingham, Taris's only sister. Might I sit down?'

'Of course.'

She sat on the sofa less than a foot away and left very little room between them, though when Bea hesitated she carried on in a whirl of words. 'I heard from my sister-in-law that you would be speaking this week on the property rights of women.'

'An inflammatory subject that I hope I will handle sensitively,' Bea returned, not at all certain of the position Taris's sister was approaching the argument from. 'I should not wish to run foul of your family.'

'Oh, I rather think it is too late for that—you have already.'

'Pardon?'

Lady Lucinda's hand swatted the air in front of her as though any problems would be easily solved. 'Asher seems to think you should be hanged, drawn and quartered for your outlandish opinions.' Her giggle softened the sentiment.

'And your other brother?'

'Oh, Taris holds all thoughts of you very close to his chest, Mrs Bassingstoke. The incident you were both involved in outside Maldon was, after all, fairly unusual, and he seldom courts gossip in any form.'

'I see.' A man who was careful, then? Careful to live his life within the boundaries of what was expected, the tittle-tattle of society dangerous to a man who would hide his lack of sight from everyone. Even from his sister? For in every conversation Beatrice had had in which Taris Wellingham was the subject, not once had she heard a whisper of what he could or could not see.

'Our family has had its fair share of tragedy, Mrs Bassingstoke, but then I would guess you are no stranger to such a thing either…' Her glance flickered to the ring on her marriage finger.

'No. I suppose that is true.'

'If I might give you a piece of advice then…' the younger woman suddenly whispered and leant forwards so that her voice did not travel '…my brother is a man who would be well worth pursuing.'

'Oh, I doubt that I would interest him, my lady,' Bea began, hating the telling blush that crept up her cheeks.

'Ahh, you might be surprised in that, for I have never seen him ask a woman to dance in years and certainly not a waltz.'

Shrewdness was evident in her eyes and because of it Bea was inclined to answer defensively. She did not wish Taris's sister to relay any tale back of a perceived interest.

'I have only recently been made a widow, Lady Lucinda, and as I am well over twenty-eight…'

'You had no children from your first marriage?' Lucinda Wellingham clamped her hand across her mouth even as she asked the question. 'I am sorry; of course that was very rude of me to ask.'

The blood pumped in Beatrice's temples as she was taken back to the house in Ipswich, the voice of her husband reverberating loudly.

I am trapped in a lacklustre pointless marriage to an uninspiring and barren wife, and all you can do is apologise?' His fist had connected with the side of her head

*before she could answer and knocked her from her chair.
'You cannot even give me an heir, Beatrice-Maude, you
cannot even give me that when God knows I have given
you everything...'*

*Everything? A broken arm and a broken nose and a
hundred bruises hidden beneath the folds of her gown...*

'Are you quite all right, Mrs Bassingstoke?' Lucinda
Wellingham's worried countenance came through the haze,
bringing Bea back to this time, this place, the wheezing in
her breath worse now than she had ever heard it.

Panicked, she tried to stand and could not, collapsing
against the sofa, a sheen of sweat marking her face and
her hands shaking.

Barren Beatrice.

Broken Beatrice.

*Such a long, long way from Bea-utiful and Bea-
witching Beatrice.*

'Should I call someone to help you?'

'No... Please do not do that...I...shall be all right.'
Clearing her throat, she made herself sit up, made herself
face the woman opposite, the curiosity imprinted in the
watching light eyes persuading her against her better
judgement to try and explain.

'I could not have children, Lady Lucinda, and it was a
great loss...'

'I am so sorry; of course, with your husband now gone
to his Maker a child might have been such a comfort. A
memory, so to speak, of all the good times, a child formed
in the mould of a man you had loved.'

Stifling a smile at such a sentiment, Bea began to feel immeasurably better. She had never met a woman who seemed so able at putting her foot in her mouth. A memory? Of love? My God, when all she wanted to do was to forget. Still, there was something appealing in such eager openness, some engaging exuberance that reality had not yet snuffed out, and so completely opposite from the careful and measured stance of her brother.

'Thank you for your kind words, Lady Lucinda. It has been most…refreshing, and please do give my regards to your sister-in-law.'

'Emerald? You know her?'

'Not well.'

'You remind me of her in some ways, not in looks of course…'

Again Bea smiled.

'But in strength. You have the same sort of intensity that she does. But now, I really must be going for I see you have much work here to do.' Her glance flicked to the pile of books and notes on the table. 'Of course, I cannot even imagine speaking in front of a whole room of people and on subjects that you seem to want to delve into…'

'And at your age I am certain I would have felt just the same.'

A practised giggle was the only reply as her young visitor stood and allowed the maid to show her out. Sitting back again on the sofa, Beatrice tried to collect her scattered thoughts. What had just happened? Had Lucinda Wellingham come to warn her or to help her?

She could not quite fathom which, for every Wellingham she met thus far was as impossible to understand as the last one and Taris Wellingham was the most difficult of them all to comprehend.

Pushing back her concerns, Bea ironed out the creases in her vibrant green-silk day dress with her fingers.

Outside she could hear the servants going about their day, cooking, cleaning, polishing. A house with only her in it. It all seemed so very wasteful and unnecessary to do such tasks each day when she was the only inhabitant, but the penny-pinching she had been forced into for so many years had led her to enjoy just a little bit of luxury.

Lord, why on earth had she told the girl of her barrenness when for ten years she had mentioned it to no one? The grief of loss turned slowly again in her chest, but with even such a small conversation the potency of such a secret was lessened. Perhaps therein lay the fortunes of the Catholic confessionals, the age-old adage of a trouble shared being a trouble halved suddenly making a sense that it never had before.

Because in all her life she had never really had friends. Not real ones until coming here to London.

Lucinda Wellingham's concern had unwittingly laid bare all the strategies she had put in place for coping.

Barren.

No wife for any man. No fit and ripe companion. No heir.

Taris Wellingham's fingers playing across her breasts, making her believe that she was beautiful and that impossible dreams could indeed come true. And between her legs the place that throbbed at the recollection of such an unexpected paradise.

'She's what?'

'Barren. She told me she was barren. Told me right out loud when I tried to console her on the untimely and unfortunate loss of her very dear husband.'

Taris felt the anger in him rise and struggled to contain it. 'I cannot even imagine what ill-thought-out plan would have taken you to the door of Mrs Bassingstoke's town house in the first place, Lucinda.'

'Curiosity.'

'Pardon?'

'You had asked her to dance at the Rutledge soirée and I wanted to see why you had.'

'Lord. Any number of reasons could have had me up on the floor and certainly none of them requiring the sort of consequences that you are now mentioning.'

'I did not wring it out of Mrs Bassingstoke, Taris. She seemed to want to tell me.'

'And who else have you told?'

'Just you.'

'Well then, say nothing of her condition to any other person.'

'I might have told Penny Whitford.'

'Might have?'

'Did. On my way back I happened to see her. She asked me where I had been.'

'God!'

'Mrs Bassingstoke did not petition my confidence on the matter, Taris.'

His sister sounded upset and he hoped that she would not burst into tears. Why the hell would Beatrice-Maude have spilled such a private thing to a mere acquaintance anyway?

Barren?

Would society be kind or cruel when the confidence she had so unwisely given became gossip?

Beatrice. He wanted to see her again, to feel her beside him, to spar with her wit and to laugh at her honesty. He would go to her discussion group on Wednesday evening and warn her of the dangers of too much candour.

Using a softer tone, he bade Lucinda to stop worrying and was pleased when she stood and took her leave.

Chapter Eight

Beatrice-Maude's salon was crowded with people and Taris hung at the back of the room beside a bookshelf, his hand against the heavy wood of it to give him balance. He rarely came to anything like this, the inherent danger of tripping always close, but Jack had accompanied him tonight and had gone to help himself to drinks at a generously laid table his friend had used much detail in describing.

The shape of someone loomed in front of Taris though he had no way of knowing who it was, so he stopped and waited, pretending to take interest in the numerous titles he had felt on the shelf.

'Good evening, Lord Wellingham.'

Bea's voice. Taris could not quite believe his luck. He moved to face her.

'Mrs Bassingstoke. I thought I should take you up on your offer to broaden my mind.'

'And I am pleased that you have done so.'

'My sister has told me that she made your acquaintance.'

Silence greeted the statement.

'Lucinda can be a chatterbox.'

Again there was silence.

'Put more bluntly it would probably be prudent not to relate any secrets into her safekeeping.'

'Secrets such as my not being able to have children, you mean?'

Taris winced at her direct honesty. 'Playing your cards close to your chest is sometimes a wiser option.'

'As close as you play yours?' The query made him wary and he jammed his hands into his pockets. No one had ever spoken to him as this woman did.

'Sometimes secrets hold us back,' she added, her husky lisp more evident today than he had ever heard it.

'Twenty-eight and a sage!' He could help neither the anger in his reply, nor the memories of her naked skin against his own.

'A barren sage,' she returned, challenge evident in the edge of her words. 'And one who it seems has forgotten the golden rule.'

'Which is?'

'In society a lady does not ever question the intent of a gentleman with a better pedigree than her own.'

'You sound scathing. I am certain such rules cannot have ever bothered you before, Mrs Bassingstoke.'

'You would be surprised…'

'But not enlightened?'

Her laugh was light and real, so different from the shallow false humour he heard in other drawing rooms of this city.

'It seems perhaps I was remiss in scolding you, my lord. Do you have a drink?'

'Jack Henshaw has gone to get me one.'

'Do try the punch. I made it myself. A non-alcoholic concoction with more than a hint of fruitiness!'

'Sounds delicious.'

She began to laugh again. 'The discussion will begin in another five minutes or so. I do hope that you will be happy to contribute.'

'I fear in this room, Mrs Bassingstoke, that my opinion will not be popular.'

'Oh, you might be surprised. The tolerance is as remarkable here as the range of opinions. Indeed, sometimes I think Parliament might do well to mimic us.'

'I will make sure to relate that to Lord Grey next time I see him.'

'Little voices can hold as much sway as more important ones.'

'A sentiment I would never question.'

'Even with the weight of privilege full upon your shoulders?'

'Such a bigot, Mrs Bassingstoke.'

Her giggles were like a fountain of joy ringing around the room and chasing away the darkness and her touch upon his arm was taken with the ease that it was given.

Not forced or obtrusive, but natural and easy.

The shadows of many people swirled around him, the timbre of voices attesting to a very large number. He did not recognise any of them. The occasional accent was of a member of the trades or a dweller from the parts of London that were considered undesirable by the *ton*, though Beatrice made no mention of occupation or their standing in society as she introduced him.

Finally they stopped and the room seemed to quieten. Whether she had raised her hand he could not tell because she had moved away from him now and Jack was once again at his side.

'The place is full to bursting,' his friend said quietly. 'Cowan is here and Lansdowne, and the wife of Lord Drummond is sitting with her sister in the corner.'

'A rather eclectic bunch, then,' Taris returned.

'With little differentiation between those who are gentry and those who are not! There are four women standing at the back who look like servants and they have a glass in their hands as everyone else here does.'

Taris began to smile. 'The egalitarianism of the Americas has come to London?'

'At least the debate on property rights should prove interesting. Some here look so formidably righteous that I hope they are not heiresses.'

'Excuse me, my lord.' Taris turned to the voice at his left shoulder. 'Mrs Bassingstoke asked me to bring you this drink.'

'Thank you.' He took the glass in his hand and sipped a fine smooth brandy. Not the fruit punch that he had expected, he ruminated, as he leant back against the wall next to Jack, listening to Beatrice call the discussion to order.

* * *

Half an hour later Taris realised that indeed this room was a hot bed of liberalism and that at least on the subject of matrimonial property rights the opinion here was swayed very firmly towards the viewpoint of the hard-done-by bride. Finally he had had enough.

'The presumptive legal unity of husband and wife can cut the other way too,' he began when there was a second of space in the heated argument, and he felt the room take in a collective breath before turning its attention to him. The heavy censure made him smile. 'With marriage a bride and groom become one person and the husband is held legally liable for any debts and civil wrongs his wife may have incurred.'

Beatrice leapt into the fray. 'I hardly think that the virtual loss of a woman's property on marrying can be compensated by the unlikely event that if she breaks a law her husband may take the blame for it.'

Taris was beginning to feel the flimsiness of his arguments, but pressed on regardless. 'Female capriciousness is well documented and some might say that the art of marriage is nothing more than an economic transaction tied to the protection of the great estates.'

A murmur settled around the room, and he realised he had probably used the wrong word when describing the changeable character of women. Beatrice's quick reply was well worded.

'Others would argue that it is nothing more than a

sham to allow men the right of power over something that was never theirs in the first place, Lord Wellingham.'

'Yet you do not take into account that economic manoeuvring favours a bride as well as a groom if the financial aspects are considered openly. The benefits of a well set-out investment can hardly be to the disadvantage of either party.'

'Well set out for the husband, my lord. Should he wish to confine her against her will and administer any properties himself he is well within his rights to do so.'

'Our world is not peopled with characters from Samuel Richardson's *Clarissa*, Mrs Bassingstoke, and the "vile Lovelace" exists only in a story.'

Laughter resounded and Taris fought to hear Beatrice's voice above it.

'Any husband may "correct" his wife should he wish to do so and the tales of such cruelty are certainly not solely the preserve of popular fiction.'

There was a tone in her voice that was not simply academic, a tone that trembled beneath the tenets of truth and chased away any desire he might have had to keep such a disagreement going.

'Touché,' he returned with a smile as he leant back against the wall and took a sip of fine brandy. 'I concede my case entirely.'

'It's not like you to give up a fight, Taris?'

Jack's question a few seconds later held a warning within it that he did not like as the chatter around them grew more general.

'You are beginning to sound just like my brother.'

'And your week is beginning to ring with the dubious clanging of firsts, my friend.'

'How so?' Finishing his brandy, Taris knew exactly what was coming.

'The first waltz, the first concession of an argument you could have won had you truly wanted to…'

'You read too much into these actions.'

'Do I, indeed? Your Mrs Bassingstoke is coming towards us, by the way, and she looks like a cat who just swallowed the cream. Perhaps your reasoning in playing the "honourably beaten" was sounder than I gave it credit for, after all.'

Taris shoved his glass into Jack's hand. 'Get me another drink, will you?'

'I will do so only because I detect your desire to be alone with the clever widow,' he returned, laughter imbued in his retort.

'Lord Henshaw looks as though he is enjoying our soirée,' Beatrice said less than a few seconds later. 'I hope that you are too?'

'The debate is all that I imagined it to be.'

Her answer was worried. 'I think our discussions go better when the opinion for and against them is more evenly divided.'

He laughed. 'You won the argument, Bea.'

'But not well. I think you gave up on me for some reason.'

He felt her hand on his arm, the pounding awareness between them blotting out all other noise.

'Could I speak to you alone? After this is over?'

'Yes.' She gave her promise easily and as the world and its noise and need cascaded again on to them she was claimed in speech by another before disappearing into the crowded room.

Taris Wellingham had spoken carefully and well in the debate, she thought. A man who was confident in his ability to woo a crowd and gracious in defeat.

He was nobody's man save his own, the one concession to his limited sight an opened hand that lay on the wall behind. He always did that, always created an anchor to the environment around him. The fence at the park, the ledge of the window in the carriage, his foot against the edge of the ditch in the snow outside Maldon.

A small habit that would be unremarkable without the knowledge that she had of how little he could really see. She watched him now from the other side of the room, watched his ease in a setting that was eminently foreign to him. The signet ring on his little finger glinted in the light as he pushed his dark hair back, his eyes creasing at the corners when he smiled.

Taris Wellingham was a man who might trace his ancestry back through all the years of history and yet he had conceded the argument to her with grace. She wondered suddenly whether he had done so by choice, as there had been a tone in his words denoting empathy that she found disconcerting.

The quick flash of her husband 'correcting' yet another

opinion came to mind and she pushed it back, all the laughter and discourse in this room as far from the big Ipswich house as she could ever be.

Lifting her glass of punch to her lips, she dragged her eyes away from the enigmatic and mercurial Lord Wellingham and wished the hour before everybody would leave away.

Everyone was gone. Almost everyone, she amended and looked again to see that Taris still sat on the blue sofa in her salon.

'I could stay if you want…?' Elspeth was uncertain as she gazed towards the room.

'I am a twenty-eight-year-old widow, Elspeth, and sense is my middle name.'

'Still, a man like that could—'

She did not let her finish. 'Look at me, Elspeth. A man like that is here merely to speak to me and I am very happy to listen.'

'You are not as plain as you might say, Beatrice, and sometimes when you argue a point so very cleverly every male in the room looks at you in the way of men who are wanting much more than just words.'

'A sentiment I shall receive as a compliment. But you forget I have no wish to take any such flattery further.'

'Very well, then. But I shall be back in the morning to make certain that…'

'And I shall look forward to the company.'

Bea was pleased when her friend finally allowed her to

shepherd her out; turning, she walked into the salon, shutting the door against the bustling of servants clearing away the last of the plates and the glasses in the dining room.

'Thank you for allowing me to talk to you privately,' he said and waited as she sat next to him.

'If this is about my conversation with your sister…'

He raised his right hand and she came to a stop. 'Did Mr Bassingstoke ever "correct" you, Beatrice?'

Her world spun in a receding dizzy arc as she clutched at the arm on her end of the sofa. Had he seen the movement? For the first time since knowing of his blindness she was glad of it.

'All my arguments were purely theoretical, my lord,' she returned, her voice sounding almost normal, 'and I could easily take umbrage should you think a man might rule me like that.'

'A lack of sight has some benefits, Mrs Bassingstoke. One of them is the ability to determine the cadence of untruth.'

She was silent.

'At Maldon you limited our liaison to just one night. I would like to negotiate for another.'

'One night…?' Her voice was squeaky.

'More if you are offering.' His smile made his eyes dance and the glasses gave him a rakish appearance. His cane lay untouched against his thigh as if, for the moment, he was comfortable and relaxed. Still, he looked much too big for her small salon, a tiger readied to pounce, the amber in his irises predatory. She could not move, could not rise and say nay to any of it, could not remember the promise that she had made to herself of 'never again'.

The clock on the mantel chimed the hour like a harbinger.

Ding…say yes!

Dong…say no!

Outside she could determine the muffled clatter of a carriage winding home in the lateness.

Ten o'clock. On a Wednesday. Already some lights in the street were out and the transport that had brought him to her door was departed. At his request?

Who indeed might know if she were again to say yes? And freedom was found not only in the choice of a good book and a night alone. Another few moments and the maids would be finished. Easy to dismiss them to their beds and then to go to hers. With him. The very idea of it made her heart beat faster.

'I am not the kind of woman to depend on this sort of arrangement, my lord. The freedom I spoke of today is important to me.'

'I am not looking to shackle you into something you might live to regret.'

At that small set-down she reddened. Of course he would not be interested in a more lasting relationship. Still, she could not quite let it lie.

'Why are you here, then?'

'Because I like you.'

She sat speechless, for such a simple and uncomplicated reason negated all the more tangled arguments that spun around in her head.

He liked her? No expectation for anything different, no change or carefulness involved in maintaining a façade that might keep him happy? The admission was suddenly as freeing as the way he had conceded his argument on property rights, his lack of malice so unlike her dead husband that it had made her almost dizzy with the contrast.

And now an offer of more, and nobody else's business save her own.

A clever man and a private man. A man who kept the world at bay so very easily.

Could she enjoy him without fear of all the other ties that drained a relationship in its never-ending complications? Simply be? Simply step into his arms and be?

'I would not expect promises.'

The smile he gave her back melted her heart.

'Of course I did not mean that you were even suggesting anything like that—' She clamped her lips together to stop the babble further.

'Bea?'

'Yes?'

'Be quiet.'

She began to laugh. 'It is just that I should not wish you to think I was easy.'

'Lord.' His expletive was vexed as he removed his glasses and laid them down on the small table next to the sofa and when his hand reached out towards her the ring he wore on his finger glinted in the light, a soldier's insignia engraved in gold.

'Tinker, tailor, soldier, sailor, rich man...' The small ditty turned in her mind. What else had he been? When his thumb traced a line from her wrist to her elbow she took in a breath and leaned back, the warmth from the fire on her face and the heat from his touch lighting a fervour more intemperate even than the naked flame.

'It cannot be here,' she whispered as his touch skimmed across the bodice of her gown.

'Then where?'

'Upstairs. If you give me time to give the servants their leave to retire.'

His fingers stilled and pulled back.

'It should just take me a moment.' But he did not answer as she stood and scurried from the room.

After dismissing the staff for the night, Bea stopped in front of the mirror above the mantel in the dining room and met her reflection.

Fervent. Excited. Basked in promise.

'No,' she said firmly. 'Do not hope...'

The thin line between her eyes reappeared and although her dimples were attractive there was much more on her face that was not.

'Just enjoy,' she said more softly before taking a breath and opening again the door to the blue salon.

Chapter Nine

Her chamber smelt of flowers and of lemon soap. The floorboards beneath his feet were slippery with polish and the rugs covering them thick. His hand reached out to the bed that he could just make out in front of him, a large square of light grey with some sort of pattern on the eider-down.

More flowers, he decided as his thumb skimmed the outline.

Suddenly he felt nervous, his lack of sight here in an unknown room more worrying than he had thought it would be. He was careful to lift his feet when he stepped around the chest at the foot of the bed.

'The fire has just been stoked. It should be warmer soon.' Bea sounded almost as nervous.

'Do you have any wine?' he asked as he sat down on the bed, the mattress squashing under his weight.

'Not in my room,' she replied. 'I could go downstairs and get it…'

He stopped her merely by catching at her arm and pulling her on to his knee.

Better, he thought, his body beginning to rise with the promise of it all. Much better, he amended, as the warm softness of breast came against him.

He had locked the door as he had followed her through and when the bells of London pealed the hour of eleven he was glad.

Hours lay before them. Hours and hours and hours. He had never before made love with a woman who knew the limitations of his sight and the relief was all-encompassing. No need to demand the candles be snuffed out or the worry of what might happen should he fumble or lose his way.

Here and now he could just be, just run his finger along the side of her face and feel her breath, her heart, the beat fast and then faster as his thumb skimmed the line of her throat, satin-soft-smooth and slender.

'Not as cold as last time,' he whispered as a log fell into place in the growing fire.

'And a lot more comfortable,' she returned, his touch determining the deep indents in her cheeks as she smiled.

Outside the wind was louder and the first spits of rain hurled themselves against the glass and for a moment he felt like a green boy, wanting her but not quite knowing how to begin, the hardness of his need pushing between them.

'I should take my hair down,' she said, the words half-way between a question and a statement and he felt her arms rise to do it.

'Let me.' His fingers ran over the silken thickness and found the hidden pins. One by one he removed them and she sat perfectly still as, clip by clip, her hair began to fall, undone and tousled, until there were no strands left up.

Beatrice sat and waited, her body coiled into tight expectation. When this was finished what would be next? Each clip marked time, loosening promise, bringing the moment nearer when his fingers might reach for other parts. With the candles still burning on the bedside table everything was so…very visible. She wished she had thought to snuff them out, to leave only the fire-glow, so kind to the many faults beneath her clothes.

And when the last of her hair fell between them his fingers traced the shape of her nose and her brow and the angled line of her cheeks.

A picture. He was forming a picture.

'I am not beautiful.' Better to say it before he thought it.

He only laughed and brought her hand to his own face. 'Close your eyes and feel me,' he said, and she did so, the shape of his nose strong, his cheek marred by the scar, his chin rough from the lateness of the day where he had not shaved since the morning.

No picture but parts. Warm. Real. For a second she knew just exactly what it was he felt and was wondrous. Opening her eyes, she saw his amber glance waver.

'Kiss me,' she said, wanting the sense of control that she had never felt with Frankwell. Her tongue ran across her lips and she pushed against him.

The dam of restraint broke completely and his mouth came down, seeking, breathing, hot and needy. She felt his hands on the side of her face and on her neck and the heat of him was like a magnet, like a centre, like a place she could not get enough of, her own tongue dancing against his, seeking an entrance, tasting and challenging, the ache in her belly a fiery red.

She could not breathe without him, she could not exist alone, her hands threading through his hair and feeling another scar bigger than the one on his face, longer, more dangerous.

Cradling her hand, she brushed the heaviness of her breasts against his fingers.

'God,' he said and then repeated it. 'You are a witch, Beatrice-Maude. I swear that you are. One kiss and I am a youth again starved of any finesse and restraint.'

'I do not wish for restraint,' she returned, the result of her words showing as a flush on his cheeks. For suddenly she just did not. This was not love but lust, and the full rein of such an emotion should not be pegged in by time or convention. Putting her hands against both sides of his shirt, she ripped it open. Just ripped it, exposing the bronzed and defined muscular chest of a man who was beyond beautiful.

Hers again! She was not careful as her fingers found his nipple and her mouth followed.

All the control that he had perfected across three years of anger broke free. This was nothing to do with what he could see or could not see. This was only about feeling and taking and the shirt that hung in tatters on his shoulders felt like a flag of freedom, a banner to release him from a heavy burden.

He could not believe how he felt, the meticulous detail of hiding his sightlessness so all-encompassing that it left little room for any other emotion. Until now. Until this minute. The shock of her teeth upon his nipple sending passion through every pore of his body.

More!

He bundled her hair in his fist and kept her there tasting until he could bear it no longer; with a quick movement he gathered her in his arms and laid her back on the bed, holding his hand against her as she went to move.

'My turn now.'

He could almost imagine he saw the smile upon her face.

She was pleased when he leant over to snuff the bedside candle, and pleased too as his fingers unbuttoned her bodice, exposing the lawn and the lace of her chemise. Unpeeled, she thought, as the cold air gave her goose-bumps, enhanced by the thought of what might come next and her whole insides tightening with delight.

He had not removed his tattered shirt, but the lacings on his trousers were gone, as were the boots he had worn. She felt almost fully dressed in contrast. The difference made her writhe.

'Hurry.' The word was out even as she thought it and

she saw the quick flash of white teeth as he drew the yellow silk of her dress down over her body. Only lawn and lace kept her from him now, and she knew he knew it too as his breathing quickened.

His hand lifted her petticoat and bundled it into a wad, before dealing with her drawers. Easily disposed of, the flimsy silk removed without exertion.

Only her now, and his hands against her thighs.

When she went to move he kept her still.

'Please?' Soft. Honest. No force within it.

She lay back again and waited as his fingers found what it was they sought and when her head arched her body followed, sweat beading the channel between her breasts as she reached for the stars and the sky and the place in her life where all was good and true and right.

'Now.' Just now. Just this time. Again. The squeezing knots of lushness washed across her, the languid ache of perfection echoing in her very bones.

Taris had never met a woman before who was so responsive, so quick to delight, so unheedful of her nakedness and pleasure.

Already she turned to him seeking, and his erection grew against the satin skin of her stomach, the bedclothes kicked away on to the floor and only firelight between them. He could see the flicker of the flames against greyness and feel the heat of passion marking the contact of her hand against his bottom. Her tongue lathed his neck, joining whispered pleadings for more.

No hesitation in it. No demand for protection or heed for safety. Just him and his seed filling her, the ease of their coupling natural and right, the rhythm of his thrusts finding a home he had never had, taken and given, deeper before spiralling up and up, his breath fast and her hips rocking and the feel of her teeth as he climaxed, her muscles milking his hardness until he collapsed against the mattress, struggling to find a breath.

Laughing. His laughter against the silence of night and the carefulness of years and the unexpected paradise of her body.

'Beatrice?' He whispered her name when he could and she whispered his back, two people caught in the question of flesh and the elation of freedom and the bone-deep rightness of what had just happened between them.

'Bea-all-and-end-all.'

And then they slept.

She could not believe that he was gone when she woke up. Could not believe that he had crept through her house without awakening her as he let himself out. How had he got home? How had he been able to negotiate a distance that he had no knowledge of? But the first rays of dawn were just touching the eastern sky and the space beside her was empty.

'Lord help me,' she whispered, the thought of her wanton abandon sending shivers of uncertainty through her this morning. Throughout all the years with Frankwell she had lain like a wooden doll on a marriage bed that had been the antithesis of what had happened last night.

'Lord, please help me,' she repeated again. Would he think her a whore? Was that why he had left? Would he think her a woman who was promiscuous and easy, a lady who would cross the boundaries without a single thought for consequences?

Consequences? Did two nights of loving mean she was now Taris Wellingham's mistress? His woman to use when fancy struck him? A lady kept for pleasure in his bedroom?

'No.' She shook her head, though a darker thought lingered. Could she refuse him should he come back? She was becoming exactly the woman she had sworn she never would be again. A woman with no say over the dominion of her own body. Last time in hate and this time in lust.

Which was better?

Frankwell at least had placed a ring on her finger and the law condoned a husband's needs in whatever form that they should take.

But now, here, in the morning light with a bed that was rumpled and musky, Beatrice felt both sullied and stupid.

A woman who would preach the doctrine of independence and then ignore every single tenet of it? She pulled the sheet around her nakedness and sat, the sight of her clothes strewn around her bed making her sigh.

Abandonment had its repercussions.

Her head fell against her hands and she wept both for the woman she had lost and for the man that she had found. And then she slept again.

* * *

Taris counted the steps between Bea's bedroom and the stairs and then counted the number of stairs to the front door.

Perfectly easy, he thought, as his hand had found the handle and he let himself out.

Jack was waiting on the front step just as they had arranged.

'It's a dangerous game you play, my friend.'

'How so?'

'Mrs Bassingstoke is a woman of some reputation. One word of this gets out and she will be ruined.'

He was quiet.

'There are houses in Covent Garden with girls whose names would not be so destroyed…'

'Enough, Jack. Where's the carriage?'

'Around the corner. I didn't wish to risk anybody seeing it.'

'Thank you.'

'If Asher learns of any of this he will have your head on the block.'

'My brother's newly formed morality is no concern of mine.'

'You hold the Wellingham name, Taris. It is simply that he tries to protect it and for a man who has rutted his way until the early hours of the morning you're surprisingly taciturn.'

'Leave it, aye?'

They walked the rest of the way in silence.

* * *

Arriving home, Taris went straight to his room and lay down on his bed. He did not change his clothes because he wanted to keep Bea's smell with him. Violets and laughter and freedom. The smell of abandonment and the joy of sex!

One hand fell over his eyes, shutting out any light at all and giving him rest.

Neither shapes nor colour. Just the blackness to think in.

He had left because he knew if he had been there in the morning things would have been difficult and in the break of day his presence would raise questions that a night-time assignation would not.

Still, he thought, perhaps he should have left something. As an explanation. Not a note, because it had been long since he had written anything in any shape and form but…something. He had not thought of it then in his haste and his worry. It was only now, when he had time to ponder and remember, that the idea had struck him. But what exactly could he have left because, lying here, he had no idea as to what his feelings were?

Beatrice was a woman who did not want a dalliance or a meaningless tryst, just as she had said time and time again that she desired nothing permanent either. Not a frivolous woman or a woman prone to a quick affair and yet not one who demanded anything else more enduring.

A puzzle. And he knew that the puzzle was linked somehow to the husband who had died only a few months back.

Corrected.

My husband said that if I ate more that I should appeal to him better.

Clues that something had not been right. He remembered Asher's words at the ball when he had said that Beatrice and her husband had not mixed much and that few people in the area had a good knowledge of them.

The town they had lived in had been Ipswich. Perhaps it was time to find out something about the late and very mysterious Mr Bassingstoke.

Three hours later with the intrusion of Ashe and Emerald and Lucinda and his mother into the breakfast room, Taris decided that his home in Kent, which was a little removed from all the other Wellinghams, definitely had its advantages. He was also glad that they would be repairing to Falder come the morrow for he felt like a goldfish might in a glass bowl, the curiosity of his family firmly fixed upon him and the questions that they asked leading to one person.

Beatrice-Maude Bassingstoke.

'Lucinda said that she was unable to have children, Taris. A sad state of affairs in a woman nearing thirty.' His mother's tone was more than critical, though Emerald seemed to be leaping to the defence of Bea.

'I think that would be an enormous sadness, Mama, and if a medical problem is the culprit then it is hardly Mrs Bassingstoke's fault.'

The wheelchair that Alice rarely got out of these days creaked as she turned it. 'I did not intimate that it was, Emerald. I only think that with such knowledge a liaison would be foolish to consider, especially if one needed heirs to consolidate properties.'

Taris stood and walked across to the window. Here the shadows were not so thick and the sun today allowed him to see the rough shape of his hand as he laid it out against the glass.

'I am not certain where you are receiving your information, Mother, but I have no intention at the moment of providing heirs for any of my properties. Ruby, Ashton and Ianthe are quite sufficient as my legally designated recipients.'

Asher joined the fray. 'You are thirty-one, Taris, and the Earl of Griffin has asked me to approach you regarding the future of his daughter.'

'A lovely girl,' his mother exclaimed, 'and so very convenient with her lands bordering your own.'

'She has few opinions on anything,' Emerald interjected. 'I doubt you would be much entertained by her company, Taris.'

'She is young, Emerald. He could teach her about the world…'

'I think she is more interested in what lies within the shops, Mama.'

'Stop.' Taris hated the impatience in his tone, but he had had enough. 'If I choose to pursue an acquaintance with Lady Arabella it will be my business.'

'She has a stable of lovely horses,' his sister suddenly said.

'I hope that Taris would not marry a woman for her horses, Lucy.' Asher began to laugh.

'Horses? Heirs? What of love?' Emerald sounded angry and a silence followed.

'I fail to see why my personal life cannot remain just that. *My* personal life.' Taris wished he had not said anything as Lucy jumped in to illuminate him.

'It's because of Mrs Bassingstoke, Taris. You seem more interested in her than you ever have been in anyone before. And she is clever and strong and most intriguing…'

'Bassingstoke?' His mother turned the name on her tongue and then repeated it. 'Not the Bassingstokes of the railway fortune? Lord. The husband had some sort of apoplexy three years ago and his wife was the one who looked after him.'

'Was it a bad attack, Mama?' Lucy asked the question, her voice low and horrified.

'Indeed, my dear, it was, and his good wife did everything for him until he died a few months ago.'

'She loved him,' Lucy said, and Emerald's answering laugh of disbelief made Taris turn away.

Love or hate, the dependence of the man must have taken a toll on Beatrice-Maude. For three whole long and lonely years?

Complete blindness would have its own need of dependency too. His hands fisted at his sides.

If he were honourable he would walk away from Beatrice and allow her to lead the sort of life that she had never had.

Freedom. How often had she said that? And meant it.

Chapter Ten

When she awoke Beatrice was sick for the third morning in a row and she tried to think what it was she had been eating lately that should make her feel this way. She always felt better by lunchtime and the malady seemed to be like no other, as with a little food she began to feel instantly better.

Perhaps it was the fattiness of the pork pies that she had started to take a liking to. She decided that she would not nibble at another piece, no matter how her body craved it.

She was suddenly thankful that Taris Wellingham had not stayed to see her in this state, and pleased as well that so far this morning her maid Sarah had not appeared.

A small respite. A little reprieve for she also knew that the servants' chatter would have alerted Sarah to the unusual fact of an overnight guest.

Drawing up the sheets on the bed, Bea tidied the room so that it was not quite so apparent as to what had been going on. She was an older woman, for goodness' sake, and should have been long past this…licentiousness.

Unexpectedly she began to smile.

Would she see Taris tonight at the Cannons' Ball? She knew that he was going for they had discussed it. Lord, what exactly should she say to him—what manner of words might sound even vaguely correct after such a liaison?

She shook her head and determined to stop overthinking things. Taris Wellingham was a friend. There could be nothing else between them and he had never, even in the most intimate of embraces, given her any cause to believe otherwise.

She was a barren widow; as a man who could have any woman he wanted, that woman almost certainly would not be her.

She should begin to go through her papers to keep her mind off things, she thought, and resolved to stop dwelling on matters that would never be and start focussing on what was.

A little after three in the afternoon, while Bea was sitting in the library reading a new book that had caught her eye, a footman came in.

'There is a man who says he was your lawyer, madam. In Ipswich, he says, and he asked if you would speak to him for a moment?' Handing over a card that was engraved with the name James Radcliff, the footman stood quietly.

'If you will show him through, Thomas, I will see him in here.'

'Very well, madam. Should I send one of the maids in with refreshments?'

'No. I do not think so.' All her dealings with any of Frankwell's lawyers had always ended in difficulty and the years of very little 'allowed' money still rankled. 'I am certain that this will only take a few minutes.'

Radcliff was dressed very fashionably as he made his way towards her, his height giving him an appearance of almost gaunt thinness. He sported a small moustache, meant, she thought, to cover the thinness of his lips. He spoke with an accent that Beatrice could not quite determine.

'Thank you for allowing me this meeting, Mrs Bassingstoke. I realise that it is most impolite of me to simply come to you like this, but I have only the smallest amount of time in London.'

'Indeed?' She could not understand why he was here and her perplexity suddenly seemed to communicate itself to him.

'Oh, I am very sorry. I shall come to the point immediately. I worked for Mr Nelson in Ipswich during the difficult years of your husband's illness, and was never quite certain as to the legality of that firm's stance on the lack of finances that you seemed beleaguered with.'

Bea's interest sharpened. Most of the Bassingstoke money had been returned to her before she had made the journey south, but according to the few records she did have there had been a shortfall. Her own desire to keep well away from the legal fraternity had put paid to the idea of having someone look into the discrepancies, yet today here in her very own home was a man who might explain them.

'You say you worked for Mr Nelson?'

'I gave in my resignation as soon as I realised the calibre of his practice, for as the son of a gentleman I could no longer condone what I saw there. I was a junior clerk, ma'am, and was seldom allowed to do anything of real value because of my inexperience, you understand.'

The whites of his knuckles showed through the taut skin as he wrenched his hands together, and Bea's eyes flicked to the closed door. It was not done, of course, for a woman to be alone with a man and a strange man at that, but the very nature of his confession was beguiling.

'I felt sure that some of the margins were not quite right, Mrs Bassingstoke, for I had seen a few things when I was not supposed to.'

'What sort of things?'

'If I were to have a guess, I would say that some of your revenue was missing and were I to hazard another guess I would say the monies were almost certainly embezzled by Mr Nelson.'

'And you have proof?'

He blushed again and shook his head. 'That is part of the reason I have come today, Mrs Bassingstoke. A friend of mine was at a discussion on the ills of piracy that you held a few weeks back and when he told me of your being here in London I decided that perhaps fate had sent me a message. I hoped that the missing numbers might lurk in the ledgers sent to you.'

'Ledgers, Mr Radcliff?' She could not remember seeing any such books.

'Books released to you on the death of your husband? Bound in brown leather, I think, and stamped with the Nelson name.'

Beatrice frowned. 'I do not recall any such thing.'

'Perhaps they slipped into your possession unnoticed.' His eyes glanced around the overfull shelves of her library. 'I would be more than happy to place myself into your service regarding this matter, ma'am, for I have always been highly thought of by the many clients I have had the pleasure to serve.'

The sound of the bell at the front door pulled Bea's attention away and she waited as another card was presented to her.

Taris Wellingham was here with his sister-in-law. Wiping down the crinkles in her skirt, she would have liked to have gone to the mirror, but Mr Radcliff's presence did not allow her this one small vanity.

This afternoon Taris was dressed all in black and he looked enormous and masculine compared to Mr Radcliff. The names of the newcomers had wrought a considerable change in the demeanour of the clerk—now he looked as though he just wanted to be gone.

'My lord.' Bea tipped her head in Taris's direction and then turned to Emerald. 'Lady Wellingham. Might I present Mr Radcliff to you.'

Taris's scowl was noticeable and she hurried on. 'He is one of the men who handled my late husband's properties.'

Emerald smiled slightly, though Taris merely fixed the man with his dangerous amber stare.

'Well, I really ought to be going,' Radcliff began as Emerald made her way over to the sofa in the corner by the fire and readied herself to sit. Taris had his hand on the back of her wingchair, his fingers splayed against the plane of the header. A touchstone. Her eyes flicked to Emerald Wellingham and the glance she gave indicated that she had noticed too.

'My maid will see you out, Mr Radcliff.'

James Radcliff followed Sarah from the room.

'For a minion of the law he seems remarkably awkward.' Taris spoke as soon as the door shut.

'He is rather a junior, I think,' Bea replied.

'Then what is he doing here? Surely a more senior partner should be sent to do business with you?'

Beatrice didn't quite know how to answer and so chanced the first thing that came to mind. 'He said that he would be pleased to help me get my affairs into order should I wish him to do so.'

When his glance met hers she blushed brightly and hated herself for doing it. Taris might not see such a reaction, but Emerald Wellingham definitely would.

His fingers against her skin and lips brushing the sensitive lobes of her ears. Whispering.

Emerald coughed once as she readied herself for

speech. 'We are here because, although Lucinda is a lovely young woman, she is also one who is rather loose of tongue. It seems she has been remiss in the keeping of your secret.'

Taris stayed silent.

Was she speaking of the secret of her barren years and her lack of children? Suddenly the import of just what they were saying began to sink in.

'I did not request her to keep quiet about this,' Bea enunciated into the growing silence, for although Taris's sister had seemed rather scatty she had also come across as a girl who did not mean harm.

'A most unwise omission, then.' Taris's voice ran alongside that of Emerald, who was far more diplomatic.

'You are more than kind in your lack of blame, Beatrice.'

'Even though it seems as if your name now is being bandied about the salons with something akin to pity?' Taris again and given in all the tones of a man to whom pity might be the ultimate insult.

'I see.' Bea could not quite, but the seriousness on both of their faces demanded at least a modicum of anxiety.

'As a result of this indiscretion, Taris thinks it would be prudent to shepherd you into the Cannon affair this evening. A buffer, if you like. Lucinda has been firmly told to stay at home.'

'By accompanying us the weight of the Wellingham name should squash such gossip back into the realm of rumour.' Taris's voice was deep.

'Even though it is true?' Bea was beginning to enjoy herself, for she wanted an absence of duplicity in this new life.

'Truth is one of those words that can be shaped to hold any viewpoint.'

'Just as privilege can,' she returned and Taris's laughter was loud.

'You do not bandy your opinions, Mrs Bassingstoke.'

'Just as you do not soften yours, my lord.'

Challenge was reflected in his amber-golden eyes. And humour. It sat on his face easily, making him look even more beautiful than he usually did.

A feeling deep inside Bea's stomach blossomed and burst into a singular ache of need. To feel him again inside her, the heat of them both melded around loving and the world dissolved into instinct. Pure. Simple. Honest.

If Emerald had not been there, Beatrice might have chanced it, might have walked into his arms and held him tightly against all the reasons why she shouldn't. But the second broke when the clock chimed the quarter hour and his attention was drawn away by it.

Emerald Wellingham stood as the last chime was heard.

'We will call by here in the carriage at half past nine. Will that give you enough time?'

'Oh, I think five hours should be almost sufficient to make me look presentable.'

Bea liked the twinkle in the Duchess of Carisbrook's eyes as she offered her hand to take her leave. 'I look forward to tonight, then.'

Taris Wellingham did not try to make contact at all as he gave her a stiff bow and was gone.

He shouldn't have let Emerald talk him into accompanying her. He had said nothing of any import to Beatrice about their hours together last night and he knew she would probably be expecting some sort of intimacy. Yet the knowledge of her ill husband's last years made him wary.

For he was another man who would need care one day! Care to do all the little things that even now were harder month by month and year by year—he didn't wish to saddle her with another dependent man.

The smell of the lawyer still lingered, unsettling him, a dark-coloured scent with top notes of bergamot. As his lack of sight had progressed, he often colour-coded people with the way they smelt.

Bea was green and fresh, Emerald the blue of the sea and Ashe a fiery orange-red.

James Radcliff's scent held a danger hidden in his early flight and his careful enunciation, the brown of his fragrance shading honesty.

Lord, perhaps the lack of sleep he had suffered last night was catching up with him. He frowned as he followed his sister-in-law into the coach, adjusting the tightness of his trousers as he sat down to mull over his most unwise longing.

Bea paid special attention to her appearance that evening, allowing Sarah to fuss over her with unprecedented patience. She even endured her maid's desire to fashion her hair into a complex pile of curls and the light touches of makeup that Elspeth insisted on were left intact when more usually she washed such indulgence away.

Tonight, however, she needed all the help that she could get and the thought of a mask between her and a society that might pillory her was comforting.

She even brought out a set of pearls that had been her mother's and fastened them around her neck, liking the way they complemented the golden gown she wore, its bodice edged in silk roses and soft Honiton lace.

When the preparations were finished and Sarah turned her to the full-length mirror, more usually left hidden behind the closet door, Beatrice allowed herself the luxury of looking and was surprised at the stranger who stared back.

No longer quite plain? Even a little pretty? The smile on her face deepened her dimples and the light caught at her hair so that the threads of other colours could be seen, sable and russet and amber, the more normal lacklustre darkness of it replaced by vibrancy.

Everything looked better. The shade of her skin, the colour of her eyes, the soft curves of a figure that had always been so very thin.

Tonight she wished that Taris Wellingham could have his sight back if only to see her, and then she shook her head as Sarah handed her a shawl of spun silver, tassels beaded with the same gold as her dress.

A fairytale?

A happy ending?

The onyx clock on the mantel struck nine-thirty just as the butler knocked on her door to announce that the Wellingham carriage was now waiting and that there was a gentleman downstairs.

Asher Wellingham stood in the lobby, his hat in hand and his gloves removed. When he saw her she fancied that he might have smiled, though the emotion was long gone by the time she had reached the bottom step.

'You are a woman who is on time, I am glad to see,' he said. 'My wife has the same habit.'

He offered her his arm and they walked outside, her shawl warm against a heightening wind.

Taris sat on one seat and Emerald on the other. Across Emerald's legs there lay a blanket of soft wool and on the seat next to Taris were others folded and waiting. For her? Chancing it, she slipped in beside the man she had thought of all afternoon.

'Oh my goodness, Beatrice, your golden gown is beautiful and the colour lifts your hair into all the shades of darkness. And the pearls around your neck…look very pretty.'

Emerald's monologue was probably for Taris's benefit, Bea thought, an inventory of the things she wore and the colours explained and as her hand reached for the blanket Taris's did the same. When she felt his warmth she pulled back and hoped that Emerald was not looking too closely, for the beat of her heart thrummed strong in her throat as the carriage started moving.

'Taris said that he enjoyed your discussion group yesterday evening, Mrs Bassingstoke.' The Duke of Carisbrook's compliment was measured.

'Then I am glad for it, your Grace,' she answered.

'Were my brother's opinions a help to you? The property rights of women after marriage are not something he has had any personal knowledge of, so to speak.'

Bea saw Emerald pushing her thigh against her husband's in a warning, but was not deterred.

'On the contrary, your Grace, he was most helpful in providing the balance to an argument that was largely one-sided. I would be most happy to have him back again.'

Taris began to laugh. 'From your reasoning, Ashe, it might be deduced that nobody can hold an opinion unless they have personally experienced the argument. Piracy was the last topic.'

Emerald squashed down a giggle and as her ducal husband turned towards the window, Beatrice got the distinct impression that she had missed out on some part of Taris's counter-claim. Leaning back into the comfort of her seat, she waited as Taris spoke again.

'If anyone should have the poor manners to make reference to Lucinda's reckless gossip tonight, Beatrice, I would suggest you shake your head and plead ignorance. Your appearance here should have set them thinking, as a guilty party generally slides off to lick their wounds.'

'Guilty party?' Emerald sounded outraged. 'You make it sound as though the whole thing is her fault.'

The Duke of Carisbrook's teeth showed white in the dimness. 'A poor choice of phrase, brother.'

'And a poor choice on Lucy's part as well,' Emerald continued and sighed loudly. 'I get less and less enamoured with society in London, Ashe. If we are not released from our duties here soon, I swear I shall take our children and go on home without you.'

'You do not live in London, then?' Bea asked, glad not to be the topic of conversation any more.

'We live here as little as we are able. Our home is near Fleetness Point at Falder Castle. From my bedroom I can hear the sounds of the sea where it runs aground on the cliffs of Return Home Bay.' She looked outside at the city all around them and sighed again. 'Perhaps you might like to come and visit us, Beatrice.'

She felt Taris stiffen beside her.

'Perhaps, one day.' Uncommitted. Distant. Two nights together and already Taris Wellingham seemed to be tiring of her company, his lack of interest when she had first entered the carriage telling and the Cannon town house almost reached.

She was merely a woman whose path had run across his for a time and in circumstances that were unusual, a woman to be protected against the errant gossip of his sister and one to whom he had unwisely given the secret of his poor eyesight. Already she could see that he regretted that, so when he took her hand as they alighted she was surprised.

'Could we walk in together, Beatrice?' he asked, the

steps in front of them many and all around people jostling for entrance. A nightmare if you had difficulty seeing. She understood why he had asked to take her arm as someone bumped against them in their haste to be inside.

Lord, how he must hate this, she thought, for even as his fingers closed over her own his face was an implacable mask of indifference. A man who would never show the world his true feelings! Bea wished that he would say something that would have allowed her some memory of last night, but he did not. Once inside people called to him on all fronts.

Taris Wellingham knew most of the names without any formal introduction and the ones that he didn't had him tilting his head in a gesture that prompted those on the end of it to supply their identities and thus solving the problem altogether. Standing with him, Bea realised his expertise at managing in his world, and also the exertion that it must take to get it right. He always faced full on to the speaker, she noticed, as though sound needed to have some sort of perspective, the tone enhanced perhaps by an equal volume?

He also made it a point to introduce her to everyone. A man who would shelter her and guard her against a careless remark or a wayward observation, and indeed by halfway through the night she thought that the plan of protection was working very well.

Until Lady Arabella Fisher approached them with a number of her friends.

Close up the girl exuded an arrogance that was less observable from further away; a beauty who would take umbrage at not being the most lauded or most visible female in the room because so many people had told her of her charms.

'Lord Wellingham,' she said, her tone honey silken and sensual. 'I did not see you at the Charltons' place last evening?'

Beatrice was amazed at the way Lady Arabella used her body as a weapon to gain his attention, but with the expected social distance of a foot or so she was also aware as to how much of what Lady Arabella did was lost on him. Still, her voice was lethal in its own right and it was directed straight at Taris Wellingham.

'That is because I was at Mrs Bassingstoke's discussion group, mulling over the problems of the world.'

Lady Arabella frowned and the other young woman near her did the same. 'I cannot believe you would miss the fun at the Charltons' in the pursuit of that bluestocking's dusty old group.'

'That bluestocking, as you call her, is right here beside me. Mrs Beatrice Bassingstoke, might I present Lady Arabella Fisher, the Countess of Griffin's daughter. Though perhaps there is no necessity for the introduction—it seems she knows you already.'

To give her her due, the girl looked highly embarrassed.

'I do beg your pardon, Mrs Bassingstoke. My manners were most rude. It is just that worrying endlessly about the cares of the world are such a burden and you can never change them anyway.'

The others around her looked every bit in agreement. Carefree and jaunty, they were all that Beatrice at eighteen had not been and for a second she was…envious. No other word for it. Envious of the years they had been allowed to just grow up. Slowly. Their rough edges polished by love rather than by anger, their mistakes sniggered over in each other's company at night and all the choices of the world before them.

Not stupid, really, but just young. Not mean, either, but arrogant in a way that young girls perhaps should be arrogant, a buttress against hardships that would come later. Something to look back upon with fondness!

'Will you dance, my lord?' Lady Arabella's question was hopeful. 'The orchestra here is very skilled.' Feeling the fingers beneath hers tense in alarm, Bea leapt in unbidden.

'Lord Wellingham is recuperating from a tumble he had from a horse,' she heard her voice saying. My God, she never lied like this, but the force of protection was stronger than the need for truth and she was glad when Taris nodded.

The irritated glance from Lady Arabella was directed straight at her as she continued. 'I have always been extremely afraid of horses for the exact same reason. Why, when I was a child, many years ago, of course, I remember my mother saying to me that it was most important to stay in a place where a steed may see you and…'

Lady Arabella listened to the pointless monologue for all of five minutes before breaking in when Bea deliberately took an overlong breath.

'I think that we really must go and find some supper now, Mrs Bassingstoke. I do hope that you will excuse us.'

Smiling sweetly, Bea watched as the young girls left. Vacuous chatter was such an effective tool to use!

'You are as formidable here as you are in your own salon, Bea. Do I now have to limp all night?'

'I am sorry, I should not have—'

He stopped her simply by holding up his hand.

'How close is the person nearest to us?'

'A few yards away.'

'If we were alone, I would kiss you.'

'And I would kiss you back.' Two could play at this game and she saw the pulse in his throat quicken.

'Hard?' His word was hoarse and an explosion of lust blossomed deep in her stomach. 'So hard that I would have to beg you to stop…'

'Beg her to stop what?' Asher Wellingham came to stand next to them and Bea bit back horror. How much had he heard?

'Beg her to stop worrying about the repercussions of Lucinda's gossip.' She had to give it to Taris Wellingham, he thought quickly on his feet.

Asher swore quietly. 'Our sister has no idea of the hurt she can cause and one day—'

'I am certain that your brother is overstating my concern, your Grace.'

'And understating my own,' Taris added, a wicked smile on his face.

The *double entendre* was deliberate and Bea was glad

that she had dropped her arm in the surprise of having the Duke overhear them.

Because at that moment in a ballroom overflowing with people and under a ceiling alight with hundreds of candles she was bathed in a feeling she had never felt before.

Exhilarated.

Powerful.

Exalted.

Not herself. Not plain and ordinary Beatrice-Maude Bassingstoke, but a woman who might attract a man such as Taris Wellingham. And keep him!

Now, clothed in gold she felt like a beautiful butterfly released from a drab and never-ending cocoon, a woman who could spar with words and be admired for it instead of hit, and one whose opinions were listened to instead of being shouted down.

When Emerald came and claimed her company she could only watch as Taris Wellingham walked with his brother towards the supper room, the pressing crowd swallowing them up before they were even ten yards away.

All Taris wanted to do was to go home and make love to Beatrice. But he had promised himself distance and honour and all of the noble attributes of a man who might care about the future of a woman who intrigued him.

The sound of gossip made him maudlin, and he longed to be in the country again. He had stayed in London this time longer than he had for all of the past eight years.

Seven days tomorrow and still he had not instructed his valet to pack.

Asher guided him towards the top of the room, where the smell of supper was stronger. 'Beatrice-Maude Bassingstoke is the most original woman here, apart from Emerald, and even then I should say they are about equal in novelty.' His voice was measured as he carried on. 'And the fact that you have been reduced to begging for a kiss in a crowded ballroom suggests a relationship different from the one you have implied…'

'You are an inveterate spy, Ashe.'

'With good reason to be so. My sources say that the Henshaw carriage was dispatched at five this morning to pick you up when you failed to return home.'

'Jack told you that?'

'He didn't have to. The Henshaw driver is my valet's brother.'

'I see.'

'Emerald too has been pestering me to ask you what your intentions are as far as Mrs Bassingstoke is concerned.'

'She knows about the conveyance?'

'No. It was the waltz the other night I think that piqued her curiosity.'

'Such a simple mistake,' Taris returned, irony in his words.

'Of course, if others find out about your midnight rambles…'

'They won't. There will be no more risks.'

'This from a man who made love with words not less than two moments ago?'

'Your penchant for nuance is legendary, Asher, as is your proclivity to exaggerate.'

'You would say it is all a lie, then?'

Taris was careful in his reply. 'I would say that I am nearing thirty-two, Ashe, and have no need to answer to anyone but myself.'

His brother laughed. 'Ahh, that is what they all say, Taris, before they fall.'

'Implying…?'

'It would take a braver fellow than myself to explain it to you.'

'Then don't.'

Silence ruled for a moment until Asher spoke again.

'Your lady has been conversing with the Duchess of Castleton for a significant time, and if Anna Bellhaven deigns to give anyone an audience for more than a minute it is generally a highly regarded stamp of approval.'

'The plan is a success, then?'

'Exactly.'

'In that case I shall leave for Kent in the next day or two.'

'Perhaps you might take her with you?'

'The Duchess of Castleton? Why on earth would I wish to do that?' His deliberate misconception had his brother slapping him across the shoulder.

'One day soon, Taris, you will wake up with a ring on

your finger and a brood of children and the knowledge that you are in the only place that you want to be.'

'Mrs Bassingstoke is a barren widow. Hard to raise a brood given that fact.'

The peal of deep laughter was distinctly unsettling and he just wished that Bea might return to stand beside him and make everything simple.

Beatrice watched Taris Wellingham from her place beside the Duchess of Castleton and the Duchess of Carisbrook.

His left hand splayed across the smooth marble on the pillar and his right held the cane. Tonight he did not wear his glasses and a lock of dark hair fell across his forehead, highlighting the amber in his eyes.

Rakish. Dashing. A man who had absolutely no idea of how appealing he looked! But it wasn't only his body that she found attractive. No, she loved the depth and breadth of his mind, with his wide-ranging opinions on anything and everything.

She wondered what his library looked like. What books he read? What had formed his ideas when he was young? She also wondered how a man raised as an aristocrat could consider other less popular ideas that encompassed a change in the perception of how society would be moulded over the next hundred years.

When the dancing began she hoped that he might ask her again. But of course he could not, given the excuse she had dredged up for Lady Arabella Fisher only a few minutes prior. She smiled, thinking it ironic that by helping him she had denied herself the chance to be once again in Taris Wellingham's arms.

The carriage ride home was full of Emerald's chatter with her husband adding his say on the highlights of the evening. Taris remained silent, lost in his own thoughts, Bea imagined, though when they reached her town house he got to his feet and helped her down the two small steps.

'I am certain that Lucy's indiscreet chatter will have been put to rest.' The wind snatched away his words even as he turned against its force, inadvertently shielding her reply from the ears of the others.

'Thank you for making certain that my reputation remained safe.' Bea could not think of even one other thing to utter. Her reputation? Last night's loving lay between them like an unspoken shout.

'Come in. Hold me. Lie down beside me and show me heaven. Again.'

Not quite what one could say to a man who looked almost desperate to be gone, and a plethora of other transports wending their way home behind him, the occupants craning their necks to watch the antics around the Wellingham conveyance.

Manners. Protocol. Exemplars and precedents. The world here was full of what was expected and what was acceptable and walking into the private residence on the arms of even a plain-looking widow in the wee hours of the morning was patently not one of these things.

'Goodbye.' His farewell contained no notion of intimacy, though he waited as two of her servants came to escort her in.

When she reached her front door and looked back she saw that the horses had already been called to walk on.

Chapter Eleven

''Tis only a hand cream that I have a need of, Elspeth. I should not wish to take up too much of your time.'

'Oh, Beatrice, it is lovely just to be walking on such a fine day. Besides, we promised ourselves an outing at the new tea shop last time we ventured out this way.'

Bea laughed. She felt surprisingly relaxed after the party last night at the Cannons'. Perhaps she had come to terms with the fact that at least in friendship she would be able to see Taris Wellingham; besides, there was little use dwelling on the sort of happy endings that she knew, for her at least, would never come to pass.

'Shall we go to the apothecary first and then—?'

Her words were snatched into a scream as a heavy shape from behind connected with the small of her back and pushed her forwards. Her arms came out to try to break the fall, but the heels of her boots had tangled with the hem of her skirt and she could not keep her balance. Tipping towards the road, the clatter of horses and the shout of a driver alerted her to the presence of danger even before she felt it, and she attempted to twist and roll away from the flailing hooves.

The wheels missed her face by a whisker, though her wrist and head hit the cobbles with a whacking crunch and the pain that radiated outwards made her feel nauseous, a receding blackness pushing away light. As she struggled to catch her breath, the shaking that she was engulfed in left her dizzy.

'Sit still, ma'am.' Sarah's voice was so insistent that she did as she said, Elspeth's sobbing behind making her wonder whether the accident was even worse than she had thought it. Wriggling her feet in her boots, she was relieved she could feel pain, for it meant that she was not paralysed.

The warmth of her maid's hand came across her own. 'I do not think anything is broken, ma'am. I think if you tried to sit up.'

Another man had now joined them and another. When Bea did as Sarah had directed and sat upright, she saw a whole group of people now ringed them. The back of her head throbbed in agony and the blood on her grazed arms soaked into her sleeves.

'Wh…what happened?' She was still shaking and her heartbeat was so fast she wondered if she might have an apoplexy and simply expire, here on this road, with the thin spring sun on her now hatless head.

'I think somebody pushed you, though I cannot be sure.'

'Can you lift m…me up?'

The two men who had knelt down beside her now took her arms on each side and carefully helped her to stand.

The weight hurt her ankle and she pressed her knuckles into the skirt of her gown.

'This shopkeeper says that you can lie down to rest in his back parlour and wait for the physician to come.'

Beatrice nodded her head, regretting the motion as soon as she did so. To get away from all the stares of a growing audience would be most appreciated.

Suddenly she felt like crying and all she could think about was that she wanted Taris Wellingham, wanted his confidence and his arms about her, wanted the feeling of safety he gave her, and his reason and his careful logic. When she was inside the parlour she would send a missive to his town house and ask him to come to her, for suddenly she did not care who might see them together, who might gossip about it or wonder. The tears she had tried to hold in fell in big drops down her cheeks.

All she wanted was Taris Wellingham to come!

The note arrived as he was about to sit down for a late lunch. Bates at his side read it out.

'It is from Mrs Bassingstoke, my lord, and there is an address in Regent Street. It says, "I have been in an accident. Hurt. I need you."'

Taris came up from his seat before the missive was even finished and called out for his butler.

'Morton. Get Berry to bring the carriage around immediately. I need to be in Regent Street.'

'But, my lord…your lunch.' Bates's voice petered out as Taris picked up his cane and strode from the room.

* * *

The shop was tiny but warm, and the blanket the wife of the furniture maker had placed over her knees was welcomed. Her hat sat on the table, a forlornly crushed shape with no hope of resurrection. The wheels had run straight over the feathers, the shopkeeper had said, and Beatrice was acutely aware that her head had only been inches away from being in exactly the same condition.

Lord, how fragile life was. A second earlier, an inch further, a grander coach or a faster conveyance and the whole outcome could have been so much different. Elspeth was still wailing noisily and she wished she would just stop, for her headache was worse.

A constable spoke to those who had witnessed her fall and Bea held her arms against her bodice, the throbbing ache easing only when she raised them up.

She felt dislocated and scared, the memory of the hooves and the horses and the violent push leaving her nervous that someone else might try to hurt her, and her shaking had not abated in the least.

A louder chatter had her looking up as Lord Wellingham walked into the shop. He came straight over to her, his hand resting on the sofa as he knelt, his cape falling into a ring of fine black wool.

'Are you all right, Beatrice?'

She could not answer, could not say even yes as a wave of relief washed across her. When his fingers came into contact with hers, she knew he could feel the terrible shaking.

'Where are you hurt?'

Because sound was such a part of how he viewed his world, she tried her hardest to answer him.

'M…my head hit the g…ground and Elspeth said the c…carriage came very close.'

He turned at that. 'Surely a doctor has been summoned?' Hard. Harsh. Impatient. 'Why is he not here?'

Watching the autocratic and imperious way he addressed the room, Bea understood power in a way she had not before. It was in bearing and expectation and in the sheer essence of history.

'He has been called, sir,' someone answered from behind.

'Then call him again. Bates?' His man stood next to him. Bea had not seen him when Taris Wellingham had first arrived in the room, but of course someone would be there to help him with the lay of the land. 'Send Liam for my physician and make sure he knows the gravity of the situation.'

As the man hurried off with his orders Bea, feared that Taris might go too and she clung to him fervently.

'Don't worry, I shall stay here with you,' he returned, and she felt his breath. Warm and real, no longer just her!

'You p…promise?'

When he placed their joined fingers against his heart and smiled, she lay back against the cushion and closed her eyes.

He was here! Now she would be safe.

Taris felt the moment that she relaxed, his fingers measuring the beat of her pulse at her wrist and finding it reassuringly steady and strong. The sticky blood he had felt on her arms was mirrored on her forehead and neck when he ran his touch upwards.

Where the hell was the doctor and what the hell had happened? A woman he presumed to be Elspeth Hardy was sobbing incessantly at one end of the room and the quiet questioning of a constable at the other told him that this was no simple accident. When Bates returned and relayed the story of Beatrice being pushed on to the road and of how she had narrowly missed being run over by a carriage, he felt a roiling sense of disbelief.

Who would try to hurt her?

Who had nearly succeeded in killing her? His anger escalated as he felt the remains of a hat on the small table beside the sofa.

Ruined like her head could have so easily been!

MacLaren's arrival a little time later took his mind from such suppositions. The family doctor had always been the sort who muttered, a trait that Taris had found useful so that he knew exactly where he was in a room.

'My lord,' he offered, and Taris felt his arm next to his, the quiet click of a doctor's tools telling him that he was measuring Beatrice's vital signs before making a judgement on her condition.

The astringent odour of smelling salts filled the space around them and then Bea's voice. Confused. Embarrassed. Flustered.

'I...I...should sit up,' she said, her fingers creeping back into his hand as she held on tight.

But the doctor wanted her to stay still and through the grey haze Taris could see that he felt around the lump on her head.

'A nasty accident. Do you remember if you lost consciousness at the time it happened?'

'I don't think so.'

'Good. Good.'

'Lord Wellingham, could you lift her and bring her out to the carriage? I think it may be more beneficial to the lady's healing to treat her at home.'

'Of course.' He was certain that the doctor had long since guessed his eyesight to be weakening, but had never in any shape or form alluded to it. Taris was pleased to step forwards and lift Bea in his arms, the presence of Bates making it an easy pathway out to his conveyance.

Bea barely moved, the heat of her body melding into his, the soft abundance of her breasts against his cloak.

When they came to the doorway she curled in against him so it was easier to negotiate the portal and once outside he counted his footfalls to the kerb. His carriage stood where he had left it and, mounting the steps, he sat with Bea in his lap.

The trip home was completed in silence, Beatrice's friend opposite sharing the seat with the doctor and Bates to his left. The small stern-faced maid named Sarah completed the party.

An hour later he was finally alone with Beatrice.

'Doctor MacLaren said you were lucky not to have

broken anything and that the grazes will feel a lot better by morning.'

'Thank you for asking him to see to my injuries, my lord.'

He heard the wariness in her tone, but he was in no mood to ignore the larger question. He also wished she might just call him by his Christian name.

'Who pushed you, Bea? Did you see him?'

He felt her shaking her head. 'Sarah said he looked like a pauper and that he ran off into the backstreets as soon as I fell.'

'A paid assailant, then?'

'I would guess so.'

'God. Who would hate you enough to do that?'

'The same person who might have sawn through the axle of the carriage, perhaps?'

Said without any artifice at all and with a great deal of frank openness. Taris stiffened as something began to tug on his mind. A smell. A certain fragrance he had noticed as he had stepped into the town house this evening. Bergamot. Scattered bits and pieces began to fall into place.

'The man James Radcliff? You said he was a lawyer?'

'The junior partner in the firm who looked after my husband's accounts. Why?'

'Has he been here again today?'

'No. I have not seen him since yesterday afternoon when you were here with the Duchess of Carisbrook.'

Such a smell would not linger, would not carry in a space for so very long. A sense of danger began to form and Taris felt as he had in Spain all those years ago before charging into battle.

Then, however, he had had all his faculties and the ability to catch sight of the slightest movement from a great distance away.

Could he protect Bea here if the man should choose to play his hand? The knife tucked into the specially made sock in his boot would help, as would the ring he wore. By turning the gold circle he clicked the edges into place and the heavy bauble changed into a lethal collar of diamond spears. Enough to surprise anyone. His cane would do the rest.

He tilted his head to listen and the silence in the house was comforting. At a guess he would say the lawyer had gone, but why had he been here in the first place? And had he come alone?

'Did Mr Radcliff ask you for anything?'

'He wanted to see some ledgers that were sent to me. He asked after them.'

'And where do you keep them?'

'Well, that is the strange thing—I do not remember having them.'

'Does your door have a sturdy lock on it?'

'I think so.' Her answer held worry and hope strangely mixed.

Standing, Taris made his way over to it and threw the bolt, testing the door when he had finished doing so.

After listening for a further few moments he crossed to the bed, realising as he came closer that she was fast asleep.

* * *

She came awake instantly and fully, with the fright of one who did not quite understand where she was or what time of day it was.

Taris sat in a chair next to the bed, his long legs stretched out before him and the stubble of lost hours shadowing his chin.

Not quite asleep. When she stirred his amber eyes flicked open, unfocused and then alert.

'What is wrong?'

When he moved his hand she saw a circle of diamond points coming from his ring. A knife lay in his lap, the other fist curled about it, easily, familiarly, in the way of a man who had long courted peril.

But as she frowned both the knife and ring were gone. A short illusion, a little fancy, and then gone; the accoutrements of battle disappearing from the everyday life of an aristocrat who walked the delicate pathways of the *ton*.

Secrets and menace and something more charged again, sensuality the other side of a dangerous coin.

The jeopardy of today's accident made risk more accepted, made the fear of rejection less concerning, made the moments she had been given with him here in the night a chance that was to be taken and not lost.

She placed her hand across his and pressed down.

'Thank you for coming today.'

'How could I not have?'

'Easily,' she answered back, years of coping alone a

burden she was more than used to. 'I thought the carriage was going to run me over.'

'As it did your hat?'

'You saw it?'

'Felt it.'

'Could the person who did it come back here tonight?'

'No.' She liked his certainty, liked the way he did not even waver. A man who would protect her against everything.

'Will you kiss me?' Hardly even a question.

'Could you stop me?' His was not either.

'I want to forget everything else save what is here, now, between us.'

'Flesh?' This time he ran his finger across her breast, easily distinguished under silk.

'And blood,' she answered, her tongue drawing a single wet trail through the stain on the skin of his hand.

'I would not wish to hurt you.'

'You will hurt me more if you do not come...'

'Inside of you?' No longer careful or limiting, the obvious stated, a balm to fright and hate and hurt.

In reply she held his finger to her lips and sucked in, the small noise thrilling and daring in a way that she had never been before.

Frankwell frowning at any enjoyment, the ghost of need always replaced by hurt.

Never again, she thought. Her body ached with the want of him, the air on her skin orange-glowed from the fire and the scars of her past disappearing into shadow, feeling and hot hard passion.

'Call me Taris,' he said. 'Call me by my name.'

She wrote it on the back of his hand, in the wet of her tongue, and saw the way the hairs rose on his arm and the breath in his throat just stopped.

One second and then two. Suspended in time and place before beginning again, neither will in it nor choice.

A small touch here, a longer caress there. The music between them was heard in breaths and heartbeats and sighs.

Their music. A symphony. To life. To living. To danger. No past or future. Just now. Risking it all.

Beatrice wished the world might stop.

'Love me, Beatrice?' Barely his voice.

She laughed as she peeled back her nightgown before taking his fingers and placing them on to the warmth.

Chapter Twelve

She was sick into the china basin kept beneath her bed and then sick again as Taris stirred.

Swallowing, she could hardly hide her embarrassment. Such a far cry from last night's loving and the first rays of dawn slanting through the gap in the curtains at her window.

Her stomach heaved again and she held back her hair, the sweat of exertion marking her skin with a glistening dew. She noticed that the grazes on her arms this morning had crusted, the first scabs of healing formed across open wounds.

Breathing heavily, she shut her eyes, shut everything out whilst she tried to find an equilibrium, the nausea receding as quickly as it had come and leaving a tiredness that was all encompassing.

'Has this happened before?' he asked when she turned towards him.

'It has,' she replied, wishing that she could have hidden it. Perhaps she was dying? Perhaps this was a sickness that had no cure, the exhaustion that accompanied the early-morning routine just another symptom of its severity. Frankwell had vomited often in the mornings in the last months of his life.

Taris didn't look happy at all. 'Hell,' he said, pulling the length of his hair back off his face. Naked, the muscles of his chest stood out along the contours of his hard brownness. 'Hell,' he repeated when she did not say a thing.

Rallying, she tried to make light of her suppositions. 'I am certain it must be something I am eating and—'

He interrupted her. 'How old were you when your mother died?'

'Seventeen.'

'And you were close?'

Bea didn't understand the meaning of such a topic change. 'Very.'

His silence unnerved her.

'Well, perhaps not as close as we had been when I was younger, but—'

'I want you to come with me to Falder. I am repairing there today and Emerald and Asher will arrive later in the afternoon.'

'I don't understand?'

'You need to be away from London.'

'Because you feel that I might have another accident?'

His laugh was unexpected. 'There are other reasons I have for asking this of you, but I would rather not discuss them here and now.'

Beatrice could not guess at what the 'other reasons' might be, but the fright yesterday had made her wary of being in the vicinity of a lot of people, and Falder with its isolated safeness appealed.

'I should not wish to be a nuisance.'

'The castle has one hundred and twenty-seven rooms! You would hardly be in the way and with Emerald and my mother as chaperons there could be no whisper of a scandal.'

Correct and careful! She wished he might have said that *he* wanted her to come, that *he* wanted to protect her, that the night they had just spent together had been the most wonderful in his life and that now he desired something more lasting…

But when she turned again he was pulling on his clothes with a haste that said he wanted to be gone.

'Bates will return with the carriage in the mid-morning and men will be sent to help with the lifting of any luggage. I am presuming that you will bring your maid with you.'

'I am hardly an invalid and my luggage will not be heavy.'

'No.' He said this so angrily that she looked up at him in surprise. 'You are not to lift anything, you understand? And do not go outside for any reason at all.'

Orders. Rules. Directives. Control.

Drawing in a breath, Bea turned away, the image of her late husband's bluster and tyranny coming to mind.

Perhaps that was what happened with men. They took

your body and wanted your mind as well. To own and shape and mould. A small interlude of bliss before getting down to the more serious business of obeying!

When she turned again he was at the door, his clothes replaced in a fashion that suggested his man Bates was close with a conveyance, his woollen cape merely draped across his arm.

'The carriage shall be back in two hours to collect you, Beatrice-Maude. Please make certain that you are ready.'

Once again back at the Wellingham town house, Taris paced up and down in the library, taking a generous draught from the brandy glass and barely believing the turn that the day had taken.

Beatrice was with child, he was certain of it. His child? He counted back the weeks to the snowstorm in Maldon because with the slight swell of her stomach he knew that she must be at least three or four months into her pregnancy.

One part of his mind beseeched the Lord that it be his, the other mulled over her assertions of barrenness and all that such a state implied.

Barren with her late husband, but not with him? He counted the time in his head since Maldon.

A few weeks past three months! Enough time for a child to swell and the morning sickness to come. How the hell could she not know that when even his limited knowledge of childbirth encompassed such information?

The answer came easily. She had been a barren wife for

all of the time she had been married, so why should the question of being otherwise occur to her now?

He felt a growing sense of worry after yesterday's accident and knew that he could not just leave Beatrice in London. No, Falder represented the only chance of safety and sanctuary and perhaps there they could fashion a plan for the future. He kicked his leg against a chair that had been left out from under his armoire and swore soundly.

Blindness.

Barrenness.

Beatrice's oft-stated penchant for independence and his own adherence to autonomy.

But a child changed everything. Everything! When the clock on the mantel chimed eleven he summoned men to bring down his luggage and walked out to the carriage.

She was ready, but she did not seem pleased. Indeed, when he took her arm to help her she snatched it away as soon as she was sitting in the carriage and placed a small bag in the space on the seat between them. Like a barrier! He could feel the leather when he brushed it with his hand.

Bates came with two maids. Both addressed him in greeting, and a new sense of quiet tension filled the space.

'It should take us about three hours to arrive at Falder. There will be food and drink supplied to you on arrival there.'

He spoke to all those present in the carriage though no one responded.

'The journey will take us east through Wickford and Raleigh.'

Still the silence was absolute.

Taris Wellingham was trying to make her feel better with his small talk, but Beatrice did not feel even remotely in the mood for chatter.

His orders from the morning still rankled, as did the way he made no mention of what had happened last night. A man who would take a relationship only up to a certain point, the control men valued more important than truth. The truth of being together and intimate, nothing held back at all.

She ground her teeth and tightly clasped her hands together, the vestige of nausea still dogging her and the lack of sleep she had suffered last night making her feel heavy and cross. When tears pricked at the back of her eyes she willed them away by taking a deep breath. Perhaps if she tried to sleep the journey would go more quickly. Ramrod stiff and upright, she closed her eyes.

Her cheek was against a hard pillow, but the soft feel of an arm holding her close made her snuggle deeper, reaching for the comfort so thoughtfully provided.

'Taris,' she whispered, thinking that the night was still before them and they had all the time in the world.

'We are almost at Falder, Mrs Bassingstoke. Perhaps now would be a good time to wake up?'

Mrs Bassingstoke? Falder? Wake up?

Horror hit her as she opened her eyes and realised the extent of her contact.

She was literally draped across him, her hand resting in his lap and her head on his chest. My God, had she snored, had she talked in her sleep, had her fingers crept where her dreams had lingered? Instantly she pulled away.

'I cannot believe that I fell asleep. I rarely do so in any conveyance, my lord.'

'Perhaps you slumbered fitfully last night?' he questioned, and she heard the humour of complicity in his words.

Ignoring it, she made much of smoothing out the creases in her skirt. 'How long was I asleep?'

'All of three hours. Enough rest to improve anyone's temper, I should imagine.'

She smiled despite the rebuke, for she did feel immeasurably better and far more able to cope. Her hat had all but been dislodged and she leant forwards whilst Sarah fashioned it into place, glad for the small interruption, though the interest in her maid's eyes was unwelcome.

'Falder should be coming into view in the next few minutes.' Taris Wellingham's voice interrupted her ministrations. 'If you look to your right, you will be able see the sea off Fleetness Point. The finger of land jutting out into the ocean is Return Home Bay.'

He did not look himself, she noticed. Memory was as potent a force as any sight and the land of your birth would be an easy recall. Still, she thought, as the peninsula he spoke of came into view, he had an uncanny ability to place himself in the landscape he was in and as her maids craned their necks to look she could not help but admire such a characteristic.

The castle was huge and rambling with turrets and gables and it dominated the grassland around it. The Wellingham family seat for centuries. She imagined what it must be like to belong to a place where your ancestors had roamed and where the family still gathered for the celebrations and tribulations thrown at them.

Taris. Emerald. Asher. Their children. Lucinda. The Dowager Duchess. What must it be like to be a part of a group of people who would see to your back and protect you for ever?

She bit down on the poignant memory of her own parents' deaths and the aloneness felt since. No one had ever looked out for her. If they had, then perhaps…? Shaking away memories, she concentrated on the moment.

A large group of servants were waiting as they pulled up into the circular drive, white pebbles clattering beneath the wheels of the carriage. She saw how Taris clasped his ebony cane and placed his fist against the handle, a habit she supposed of realising the exact moment when they stopped and when the door might open.

Always in control. Always cognisant of the slightest change in circumstance so that he would not be surprised.

The old man who opened the carriage door looked delighted by Taris Wellingham's arrival.

'Master Taris.'

'Thompson.' Instant recognition and his hand thrust forward. 'I trust you are faring well up here.'

'Better than in the city, my lord.'

'And your wife, Margaret. Is she keeping well?'

'Indeed, my lord. I will tell her that you asked after her.'

Another man strode up to join them and the same sort of conversation ensued. Taris Wellingham was a lord who would take the time to know old retainers on a familiar basis. Frankwell had never made an effort to learn the name of even one servant and consequently there was a never-ending stream of them through the house. Another thought occurred to her. Perhaps the ploy had been deliberate on his part to keep her isolated from any friendships? Loyal servants might have bolstered her revolt and led her to believe the fault did not lie entirely within her.

How naïve and stupid she once had been. That was the worst of it. The knowledge that a man had kept her so trapped and down-trodden made her feel diminished and guilty. A woman with a secret of shame.

Following Taris down the line of servants, she was surprised when he stopped and brought her to his side to make introductions to the housekeeper and the head butler. This was what a husband might do when first bringing a wife to his family domain, and she was hardly that. The strangeness of it all was confusing and she was glad when they walked up the front steps and came inside.

The entrance hall was beautiful. A wide staircase wound its way from the ground to the first and second floors, the banisters of old polished oak. Off the hall to all sides were numerous doors.

When one opened suddenly she saw an old woman sitting in a wheelchair, a blanket across her knees and a very fine gold-and-ruby necklace resting in the folds of her heavy woollen gown.

'The Dowager Duchess is waiting in the blue salon, my lord.' Bates's voice was quiet and as he walked away Bea was surprised that Taris turned her aside with a whispered confidence.

'My mother can be a little overpowering sometimes, but as she is old I usually humour her views.'

'You sound worried that I might not.'

He laughed. 'It is not her I am trying to protect with such a warning, Bea, but you.'

'I am not a green girl…'

'She has some knowledge of your past.'

'Oh.' The wind was quite taken from her sails and where interest had been before, there now lingered dread. How much did she know and who had told her?

'Mama.' Taris leant down to kiss her forehead. Here in Falder Beatrice noticed his new ease of movement. He had even placed the cane at the front door with his cloak and hat.

His mother's hands came across his and she held them close, the look on her face one of love and then considerable interest as her gaze fell behind him.

'And you have brought a visitor…?'

'Mama, may I present Mrs Beatrice-Maude Bassingstoke.

Beatrice, this is my mother, the Dowager Duchess of Carisbrook. I have asked Beatrice down for a few weeks in the hope of showing her Falder.'

'I see.' The woman's eyes slid across her face, missing nothing. 'I was sorry to hear of the recent loss of your husband, Mrs Bassingstoke.'

'Thank you.'

'My own husband was incapacitated for his last few years and I know how very difficult it can be.'

Beatrice nodded.

'Did you have much help with him?' Inside the question Beatrice sensed knowledge.

'I did not, Duchess.'

'No mother or father? No sisters or cousins?'

She waited as Bea shook her head.

'No one?'

The silence stretched out until the old woman gestured her forwards. 'Then you are in need of a good holiday, my dear. A long overdue holiday, I should imagine. Do you play whist?'

'Badly.'

Taris's mother began to laugh. 'Emerald told me just the same. Do you like the sea too?'

'I beg your pardon?'

'The sea. Emerald enjoys the ocean. I was wondering if that was some other thing you had in common?'

'I have not had much experience of water, Duchess.'

'Horses, then? Do you ride?'

'I used to ride well once, but—' She stopped.

'Then you must do so again. Taris has a number of his steeds standing at Falder. He will help you choose an appropriate mount. What of dancing? Are you a woman who enjoys a whirl on the floor?'

Before she could stop herself Bea reddened rather dramatically, thinking of the one and only waltz she had danced in her entire life. And then she took in a breath. My God, this woman would think she was a dolt should she keep up with this tack. 'I read extensively, Duchess, and write too.'

'Novels?'

'No. Tracts for *The London Home*, a new broadsheet for women exploring various options that they may wish to take in their lives.'

'Making up for lost time, then?'

Taris interrupted her. 'It is getting late, Mama, and we need to refresh ourselves before dinner.'

'Which room has the housekeeper placed her in?'

'The green salon at the top of the stairs.'

'No, that will not do at all. Put her in the gold room, for it is far more restful. She will like that room better.'

Taris's smile broadened. 'You are sure?'

'I am,' she said curtly before turning away, the first surprising beginnings of tears on her lashes.

Once again out in the hall Bea was not certain if she should ask Taris anything about the exchange; when he did not seem to want to discuss the conversation further she merely did as the housekeeper asked and followed her. Taris stayed below, watching her as she made her way up.

When they finally came into her chamber Bea thought that she had never in her whole life seen such a beautiful space. It was as though light and airiness had been spun into the fabric on the bed and the walls, a deeper brocade in burgundy counter-playing against it. A writing desk inlaid in patterned walnut was set up near the window with pen and paper and ink, and a bookcase graced the whole of one side, the titles numerous and varied.

Long full-length glass doors opened out on to a balcony and away far in the distance the forests climbed up the hills, moving from lighter green into darkness.

'Dinner will be in three hours, ma'am. I shall send your maid to help you dress.'

'Thank you.'

'Master Taris said to tell you that he would come himself to bring you down to dinner.'

'I shall be ready.' When the woman turned to the door Bea could temper her puzzlement no longer. 'Might I ask you a question before you go?'

'Of course.'

'This library looks as though someone has spent a great deal of time building it up?' Her fingers slipped across the bindings of the books.

'This was Master Cristo's room, ma'am, before he left for Europe.'

'Master Cristo?'

'The youngest Wellingham brother, ma'am.'

'I see.' She waited as the woman departed and looked closely at the titles. Older works with little that had been published during the past few years. Cristo Wellingham? She had not heard this name mentioned once in society and resolved to ask Taris all about him.

The door flung open less than a half an hour later and Lucinda Wellingham stood there in her travelling garb and a look of wonder on her face.

'It is true, then? Mama allowed you to stay in here. My God. No one has been in here since—' stopping, she put her hand to her mouth '—since Cristo left.' Beatrice was certain that this sentence was far from the one she had been going to say. 'Mother must have really liked you.'

'I think she wanted me to have the room because of all the books. I had just told her that I both read and write.' Another thought struck her. 'Did the Duke and Duchess of Carisbrook travel up with you?'

'They did. We came in two carriages as the children and their nanny were with us and so was Azziz, Emerald's friend from when she lived in the Caribbean.'

'She lived in the Caribbean?'

'For years and years.'

Lord, Beatrice thought, every new thing she found out about the Wellinghams made the family stranger.

'Have you travelled, Mrs Bassingstoke?'

'No. I had been to London a few times years ago but of late…no.'

'The Wellingham ships travel all over the world. One day I shall take passage and stay away for years. You and Taris could come too and we could see the sights together.'

'That is very generous of you, Lady Lucinda, to think to include me on such a grand scheme, but—'

'Taris likes you or he would never have brought you here. He never has, you know, brought anyone else. You are the very first.'

Hesitating, Bea wondered just how much of her recent incident on Regent Street she should relate to a young woman who talked a lot. 'Have you spoken to your brother about why I am here?'

'No?' Interest was rife.

'Then perhaps you should.'

'He used to be easier to talk to than he is now. His eyesight is worsening, even though Asher forbids anyone to mention it, and I think Taris worries he may be a burden. To everyone.'

For the first time since she had met Lucinda Wellingham, Bea saw the kernel of a profound truth in her utterings.

A burden? Did he think he might be such? To her? Another worry surfaced. He knew a little of her nursing a sick husband. Did he put himself in the same category?

She wished she might have had the courage to ask Lucinda Wellingham just how the accident to his eye had happened, but it felt too much like prying to make a point of it. Besides, a quick knock on the door had them both turning and Emerald swept into the room, a child of about one in her arms and a smile on her face.

'Bea? I had heard you were here. How wonderful. I can't wait to show you Falder and you can meet the people from the village and my aunts and cousin.'

The little child suddenly twisted and reached out and Emerald laughed as she deposited the red-headed mite into Beatrice's arms.

Beatrice had never in all her life been close to someone so young and the experience of having small hands reaching out for her was amazing.

'Her name is Ianthe, and she's almost a year old.'

'Ianthe?' Bea turned the unusual name on her tongue. 'After the daughter of Oceanus in the ancient Greek?'

Emerald smiled. 'You are the first person to have ever asked me that.'

'The Dowager Duchess has just finished telling me that you enjoy the sea. It was easy to make the connection.'

Ianthe cooed as Bea wriggled her fingers. Then the child grasped on tightly and put them into her mouth.

'She's teething and wants anything at all to chew.'

Bea felt strong gums gnashing against her skin, and then felt the beginnings of a tooth protruding, and a great wave of happiness swamped her in its intensity. Being at Falder in a golden room with Lucinda and Emerald beside her and a baby in her arms felt like a wonderful gift. The gift of other people's lives where years hadn't been lost to silence and fear and where her company was sought out rather than rebuffed.

Tonight she would begin a journal and write everything down, and then when she was back in London at her town house she could read the passages and remember what it truly felt like to belong.

Chapter Thirteen

Dinner proceeded in the same fashion as her afternoon had, all laughter and teasing and talking. Azziz, Emerald's friend, was a large tattooed man with one ring in the remains of his right ear and a number of white scars across his hands. The same sort of scars she had seen on Emerald's hands.

At his family table Taris gave as good as he got and Beatrice listened to his explanation of the newest farming methods with admiration.

Asher's talk was mostly about the building of a new ship.

'She's due out to India in four months' time, Taris, and you said you wanted to be involved in the maiden voyage.'

'I doubt if I can get away.'

'But you had it all planned!'

'I know, but something else has transpired.'

'Something such as…?'

Taris did not answer and a slight awkwardness filled the room, though it was dissipated by Lucinda when she knocked over her wine and sent that end of the table into a flurry, until the footman mopped it up.

Taris was glad when his brother dropped the subject of the journey out to India. He could not go because the child Beatrice carried would be almost born and there was no trip in the world that would justify missing the birth of a son or daughter.

A cousin for Ruby, Ashton and Ianthe, missing pieces of the Wellingham family puzzle falling into place. Tonight Beatrice was beautiful. To him. Beautiful in the way of a woman who did not know that she was, no vanity or artifice in it, her husky lisp answering questions and giving opinions and laughing at exactly the right time when Ashe chanced a joke. He imagined her dimples deep shadowed in the light, and her leaf-green eyes and the swell of bosom above the silken creation she was in.

He felt the unseemly rise of his sex beneath the table as he mulled over the chances of being accepted into her bed tonight. Cristo's rooms were easily accessed from his own and he was pleased about his mother's unexpected intervention.

The thought that perhaps the sleeping arrangements had not been as coincidental as they appeared did cross his mind, as he had spent a greater part of the past two hours fending off questions from Lucinda and Asher about his relationship with Bea and her presence here at Falder.

Beatrice was speaking now on the topic of banking, proposing that country banks be monitored by the Bank of England, much to the delight of Emerald and the chagrin of his brother.

'The panic for cash is hardly the fault of the country

banking system, Mrs Bassingstoke.' The tone in Ashe's voice was firm, but Bea replied quickly.

'Oh, I disagree, Duke. When people lose faith in an institution's ability to meet their obligations, one would imagine Parliament would elect a stronger body to step in and lay down stricter rules.'

'I have always favoured a less vigorous approach—'

Emerald did not let him finish. 'Because he is a partner in a number of the country banks.'

'A vested interest, then?' Beatrice continued, her tone full of a feigned rebuke. 'Making it harder to be impartial?'

'Two against one is a difficult way to win any argument,' Ashe parried, 'though if you had supported me, Taris, we might have managed it.'

'After my last public drubbing at the hands of Mrs Bassingstoke, I dare not risk another one.'

'Public drubbing?' Lucinda had joined the fray. 'Oh, do tell us of it, Beatrice.'

'The argument that your brother refers to was hardly a good example, as I always felt that he lost it on purpose.'

'On purpose?' Her suspicion was so evident that Taris began to laugh, though his mother was nowhere near as amused.

'In my day well-bred young ladies went to all lengths to stay out of any argument not pertaining to the running of the marital home.'

'We have come a long way since the 1770s, Mama,' Lucinda managed.

'Thank goodness!' Emerald interjected. 'Besides, women these days are encouraged to have an opinion on whatever they fancy, Mama, and it would be most unwise not to take up such opportunity.'

Taris felt Asher move beside him. 'A Wellingham man would not swap a feisty wife for all her weight in gold.'

'Or all the money still left in the besieged country banks.' Emerald laughed.

Bea watched as the Duchess of Carisbrook smiled down the table at her husband. A woman who was happy in her world and cherished. For her opinions and her debate, for her originality and her arguments.

And right then, at that very moment, something thawed inside Beatrice. Some icy guilt that had insisted her husband's intractability was somehow her fault. That she deserved punishment for not being pretty enough or interesting enough or barren.

For twelve years she had laboured under a false premise and a dreadful error. For twelve long years she had obeyed and submitted and conformed.

Tears filled her eyes and she stood, excusing herself from the table under the pretence of feeling ill. If she stayed, she would embarrass everyone, for her long held-in tension was finally demanding release.

Taris heard her sobbing as he opened the unlocked door. Crossing the room, he felt her shoulders shaking and the tears on her cheeks as he held her close.

'Shh, it may not be as bad as you think.'

'I…am…sorry,' she said, when the tempest seemed past. 'Rudeness is something that should never be excused and your mother will not be thanking me for my strong opinion at the table.'

'You think you were being rude to offer an opinion? My God, Beatrice, if you cannot say what you think, how could you live?'

When she burst into tears again Taris knew that he had said the wrong thing.

'I did…didn't live,' she whispered after a few more moments. 'I was always…scared…of him.'

'Your husband?'

She nodded and her whole body shook. 'He would hit me if I did not say the right thing.'

'God.' He pulled her closer.

'He would hit me and hit me and hit me.'

Her heart raced at twice the normal pace and made Taris want to find the dead man and strangle him anew.

'I have never told anyone that. Not anyone,' she repeated.

'Then I thank you for telling me,' he replied, liking the way her fingers buried themselves beneath his jacket as though his warmth was her sanctuary.

'But I won't be that way again,' she vowed a few moments later when she had collected herself. 'If I think something is wrong, I will always say it.'

'Good for you.'

A teary half-laugh ensued. 'And I will read books in bed till after midnight should I wish to.'

'Would you read them to me?'

'Yes.'

'In bed, you say?'

She laughed again. 'Thank you for bringing me to your family home.'

'Falder has a legend that insists those who love the place will always return.'

Return!

Bea smiled into the superfine of his well-cut jacket. Taris's voice was soft and his hands were gentle, the fire-light on his hair showing up the darkness.

A good man. A strong man. A man who walked his world with the certainty of one who was both moral and ethical.

She loved him. She did. She loved Taris Wellingham with an ache. The realisation hit her like a lightning strike.

My Lord, she had fallen in love. Hopelessly! Desperately! Completely! And she dared not tell him any of it.

Tell him and risk the end of a friendship.

Tell him and see pity where respect now stood.

Tell him and know that he would never love her back.

Her stomach heaved in a new bout of rising nausea and she swallowed heavily.

She needed time to regroup, to understand the implications of what was happening between them and to protect herself.

'I would like to rest now….' She left the ending unfinished and saw the flick of uncertainty as he realised she wanted him gone.

But he went. Without anger or shouted words or recriminations. A different man completely to Frankwell.

* * *

Taris walked around the gardens, not trusting himself on a steed at this time of night. He would have liked to have saddled up Thunder and run across Falder with the wind in his face and the stars at his back just like he used to. He would have liked to gallop to the highest hill above Fleetness Point and shout at the sky. Shout with anger and pain and agony, not for himself but for Bea. For a younger Bea. Trapped. Fearful. Silent.

But tonight he could only walk fast around his mother's garden, the fence along the edge keeping him to a pathway, coriander, rosemary and thyme pungent when his cane brushed the heads of the cuttings his mother had nurtured.

Behind him he heard footsteps.

'You look like a man who is wrestling with demons.'

Ashe's voice.

Taris shook his head. 'Not demons, but truth.'

'An even trickier adversary.'

The wind in the elm trees on the ridges wailed across silence.

'Emerald thinks that Mrs Bassingstoke might be with child. Could it be yours?'

Taris looked up, trying in the greyness to see anything of his brother's face and failing. He remained silent as Ashe kept talking. 'Beatrice reminds me of Emerald. She has the same steely determination and the same vulnerability.'

'Her husband hurt her badly.' Taris hadn't meant to say it but the secret was too new and too raw to keep in.

'Hell.' His brother's shock underlined his own, making him feel better.

'She spent twelve years married to a bully. Now all she wants is independence.'

'A difficult ask.'

'I know.'

'Tread carefully, then, for I like her and Emerald is determined she wants to keep her.'

Taris knocked on Bea's door and she answered it very quickly. He felt the heat of her room against his face and smelt violets.

'May I come in?'

'Yes.' No hesitation in her assent. He heard the rustle of her nightwear as he followed her inside. Satin, probably. He wished he might have been able to run his hands across the garment and know. But he stood still instead.

'We need to talk, Beatrice-Maude.'

'Because you would like me gone?' Fear threaded her reply.

'Gone? Lord, Bea.' He reached out, palm up, and was pleased when he felt her fingers steal into his. A contact. Drawing her closer, he could feel the satin was cool and her hair tickled against the bare skin on his hand. Long and heavy, she had let it down for slumber. The thought made him take in a sharp breath and he scarcely knew how to start.

'When we made love at Maldon, Beatrice, I did not protect you against the possibility of a baby.'

'With my history it does not matter.'

He smiled into her hair and wished that he could look into her eyes. Really look.

'I think that it might have mattered…'

She pulled back, but he did not let her go.

'Marry me.'

'No.'

'No?'

'I cannot marry you.' Her voice was shaky. 'Last time I married a man who did not love me I learnt the mistake of that.'

The air around them was charged with question.

'Love?'

The way he said it was like a dagger to Bea's heart. Love was not something to be considered or questioned. Love was simply a knowledge, unconscious and untempered.

She felt the nails of her fingers dig into the skin on her forearm.

Love me. Love me. Love me.

But as the silence lengthened she knew that he would not say it, could not say it.

'I have enough money to disappear, to make a new life. You need not feel hemmed in by a simple mistake.'

'Mistake?' he countered. 'You think this child is a mistake?'

'This child?'

'Our child.' His hand fell to her stomach. 'You must have known.'

Bea shook her head.

'Your sickness in the morning...'

She shook it again. 'No, that can't be. I am barren.'

'With your husband that might have been the case, but with me...'

'Pregnant?' She could not go on. The word quivering between them like a barely believable truth!

'Ahh, sweetheart.' He stood, not touching, but only a breath away. 'You did not know?' Gentle sorrow tempered his question. 'I thought that you must have known.'

'I thought I was ill.' Tears blurred her eyes, but she willed them back. 'I would not hold you to any promises.'

'It is too late for that, I think, with a new life growing.'

His finger ran up her arm and then across her cheek and settled on the soft skin of her forehead. 'Where in all of this lies the place for compromise? Is it here?' His hand fell lower. 'Or here?' he questioned, as the beat of her heart began to thud. 'Anything could be possible...'

She should have said nay. Should have loosed his hold and stepped back. Should have said that the joining of their flesh was only a fleeting thing, ephemeral and unimportant. But she could not say that and mean it, as his warmth spread across her, increasing her desire, and the man who was the Lord of Darkness lifted her in his arms and took her to bed.

He was not there when she woke, the warmth in the sheets long gone. So she lay with her hands across her stomach, trying in the silence to listen, to understand and believe that another soul lay within her, waiting for its own chance at life.

A child. A Wellingham child. A child conceived on a

snowy night when the old fetters of restraint had been washed away and freedom left in its place. She smiled and wondered if tears were the preserve of impending motherhood as a warm wetness ran down her cheeks.

Victory.

Finally.

And so unexpected.

Joy juxtaposed with worry. Would Taris now feel bound to her in a way he might not have otherwise?

She shook away the idea as nonsense. A family. Home. Unity. Love. She could not turn away from this astonishing second chance.

When she came downstairs after eleven o'clock she learnt that Taris had taken the carriage for Ipswich and would not be back again until the morrow.

Emerald had given her the news as she sat at her own breakfast.

'Perhaps he had some business that could not wait to be attended to?'

'Perhaps.' The poached eggs on toast that she had selected were suddenly very hard to swallow.

'May I offer you a piece of advice, Beatrice?' Emerald's look was measured. She waited until Bea nodded.

'The Wellingham men are hard to catch, but very easy to keep. Once they love, they love well.'

'Taris does not love me. He has never said it.'

She blurted the truth out like a green girl, though Emerald's smile unnerved her.

'Taris was an intelligence officer under Wellington. For years he scouted across Northern France and Spain under the guise of one from those climes and never once was he unmasked. Did you know that he speaks fluent Spanish and French and was one of the finest marksmen the army had ever seen?' Stopping, she took a sip of strong black tea. 'When he came to the Caribbean to rescue my husband from the clutches of a pirate colony…' Emerald noted Bea's surprise at this revelation '…he was the only man to have ever discovered their lair and the only man to leave it on his terms. The bullet hit him as he dragged Asher out into the sea and to safety.'

'A bullet?'

'His sight was damaged when he saved my husband and because of that I owe him everything!' She leaned forwards. 'Give him a chance to know what it is he thinks. Give him the same knowledge that I had to give to Ashe.'

'The knowledge?'

'That he cannot live without you.'

Bea pulled back. 'I do not think…'

Emerald's fingers covered her own.

'Taris has a need to understand that the man he is now is the one you want, not the one he once was. He needs to redefine himself and only you can help him do that.'

'By loving him?' Finally Beatrice saw where she was going with her argument.

'Exactly.'

Chapter Fourteen

The talk with Emerald turned her sadness into something different altogether.

Challenge now fired her imagination and the new ruthless single-mindedness was as freeing as it was unexpected. By the next evening she was watching for Taris to return to Falder, the plan in her mind fully formed.

She had borrowed from Emerald a nightgown of lace and silk and the violet attar she wore had been sprinkled liberally over it. Around her bed candles fluttered, the scent of flowers vivid in the wax.

Now she had a need of only the man himself, though as the hours raced on into night she began to think that he might not come at all.

Bates had assured him that the light was still showing beneath Beatrice's door, though Taris knew the hour to be past twelve. Thanking his man, he waited as his footsteps receded and lent against the wall to mull over his options, for his talk with the solicitor had confirmed his own suspicions.

He had spent the day in Ipswich after contacting Beatrice's lawyer, Robert Nelson, and the man had had a story to tell that had been entirely different from the one James Radcliff had told.

'I trusted the young man and all I was repaid with were lies. If I were to see the scoundrel again, I'd have a few choice words to blister his ears with before I set the police upon him, I can tell you that, for it seems that he had been siphoning off rightful money for all of the three years he was in my employment and withholding funds from Mrs Bassingstoke with her husband so dreadfully ill.'

'And the ledgers you talk of. Where are they now?'

'Not here. I have looked high and low for them—if we can lay our hands on them the proof will be irrefutable.'

Suddenly things began to make more sense to Taris. 'Did Radcliff know that he was under suspicion?'

The man nodded.

'Lord.' If Radcliff had thought the books were with Bea in the carriage he might have sawn through the axle in an attempt to reclaim them. The accident in Regent Street could have been his doing too, for the scent of the man had been in the house when they had returned. Perhaps he had paid an urchin to create an incident, giving him the time he needed to visit her house. Without the ledgers any case would be far harder to prove and paper was easily destroyed. Danger began to mount, for time would only sharpen a man's desire for what it was he sought, especially one with blood on his hands and a future that was at best uncertain.

Returning to Falder to see if Bea stayed safe was suddenly vitally important, for if there was any risk to her at all…

The memory of her refusal of marriage still rankled and the walls he had put up against a world that was becoming increasingly darker seemed more of a prison now than a fortress. Isolation and exile had their drawbacks and his inability to be honest was one of them. Still, years of coming to terms with his loss of sight could not be easily translated into acceptance and it had been a long time since he had ever let the more frivolous emotions of love and trust take over from caution and denial.

He wanted back what he had been and knew that he could never have it. He doubted he could hit a target now at ten yards, let alone a hundred, and even the smallest trip to town involved the eyes of his man Bates. Always dependent, never alone.

He laid his hands against Bea's door. The only place he felt truly himself now was with her, curled beside him in the darkness, feeling the soft truth of comfort and knowing the fineness of her mind and the generosity of her body.

Home.

With Bea.

The thought struck him sharply, piercing all the defences he held in place. No longer just himself.

The smell of violets wafted close as he pushed open the

door. And perfumed wax? Candles, he determined, the warmth of flame felt even from this distance. So many?

Beatrice's soft breathing from the sofa had him turning, puzzlement at her slumber and anger at her forgetfulness in not dousing the wicks. When his fingers touched warmth he wondered what it was that she wore, lace and skin in equal measure along the fine lines of her legs. Like the garments a courtesan might wear in the better establishments off Curzon Street.

He knew the instant she came awake.

'I fell asleep?'

'It is well after twelve. Why did you not seek your bed?'

'I was hoping that you might come.'

He sniffed as she moved, the scent of violets almost overpowering. Much more potent than usual! 'Did you spill your bottle of perfume?'

'No?' The word came back to him as a question.

'There is strong smell of violets in the room.' He crossed to the candles. 'And it is dangerous to leave so many candles alight whilst you slumber, Bea.'

She laughed easily, but ceased the instant his hands covered the full abundance of her breasts. He loved the way she did not pull back.

'What is it that you are wearing?'

'A nightdress that Emerald lent me.' The shyness in her voice was easily heard as she explained. 'I have been waiting for you to return home.'

Suddenly he understood. 'This was all for me? The candles, the perfume, waiting up...?' Taris felt something inside himself that was foreign and unfamiliar and disturbing. Something undeniable. Something so empowering that the very essence of it made him still.

'Emerald told me a little of your time in the army under Wellington. She said that you were a master of disguise who never once was caught.'

'That was a long time ago and I was a different man.'

'Have you forgotten the languages Emerald insists that you speak fluently?'

'No.'

'And are you not still involved in the deciphering of ciphers for the British Army?'

He smiled and the amber in his eyes was dancing light. 'Yes, but if anyone else knew that you knew I'd undoubtedly be instantly dismissed.'

'You negotiate a world that every other person might simply have given up on, Taris, and that to me is heroic.'

He stayed silent.

'The lace on this gown is almost silver and I am wearing nothing at all underneath it. My hair is newly washed and scented and the nails on my feet and hands have been very carefully painted. Pink,' she added, as though the colour might be important to him. 'And I have done none of this to entice a man whom I pity or patronise. Frankwell abused me for years, you see, and the scars that I bear are the scars of shame and fury. Fury that I did not fight back or seek help or say what it was that was happening to me. Your scars, on the other hand, come from honour and valour and bravery, wounds that tell the story of saving your brother and escaping from a place that no other ever had before. If I could exchange my damage for yours I would, Taris. I would do it in a second.'

Her voice broke on the last words, but she did not let him speak.

'I would exchange it because you never gave up as I did.'

'Never gave up.' The echo of the words nearly broke his heart. For him and for her, two people dealt a hand that was not fair, yet surviving in spite of it. Or perhaps because of it? The question surprised him.

Brave and valiant? In her eyes he was that?

Outside the wind was loud and the first drops of rain had begun to fall. Inside with the fire and the candles and the cobweb nothingness of a gown he had no need for sight to imagine, a new possibility began to dawn on him.

Home and hearth and Beatrice.

His hand stole to the slight swell of her stomach and he felt her quick intake of breath.

And family. His family. Children and laughter. More than one. Many. Running at Beaconsmeade and Falder and knowing the land as well as Ashe and he ever had.

'This child will be born in less than five months by my calculations and I should not wish it to be born out of wedlock.'

She did not speak.

'Would you give me leave to court you, Beatrice-Maude? Court you properly, I mean?'

'Properly?'

'Partner you to the country entertainment on offer

around Falder? Court you in the way of a beau who has only the very best of intentions?'

In response she entwined her body around his, leaving him with no doubts as to her answer.

All his reserve broke. 'Love me, Bea,' he whispered into the long curtain of her hair.

'I do,' she replied and his heartbeat surged. Nothing could have stopped them coming together and like dry kindling to a flame they rose before floating down spent, breathless with ecstasy and repletion and release.

'I love you, Taris.' Said again as he closed his eyes and slept.

Taris could tell that the gossip of the servants had come to the ears of his brother when he walked into breakfast with Beatrice the next morning.

'Did you sleep well?' Humour was apparent in the question and he was certain that Bea had heard it too.

'Very, thank you.' Determined that he would not let Ashe have his fun, he helped himself to a generous plate of eggs and bacon and began to speak of the Davis function that they had all promised to attend that evening.

Emerald's arrival, however, only seemed to add to the tension. The escapade with the nightgown had probably been her suggestion in the first place and as she sat he could tell that the meal was going to be a long one.

'You arrived back late last night, Taris?'

'I did.'

'And you are late rising this morning?'

'*I* am.' He stressed the personal pronoun with a telling emphasis.

'Which is unusual for you?'

'It is.'

'Mama thought she heard music coming from Cristo's room last night. She told me so this morning.'

His sister-in-law could no longer hold in her laughter and it settled around the room. Beneath the table Taris felt Beatrice's hand steal into his own and she squeezed it before speaking.

'Where is your brother Cristo?'

Her question was exactly the right one—it drew everyone's attention into a completely opposite direction.

'Our brother has lived in Europe for a number of years after deciding that England no longer suited him.'

Asher's reasoning was not quite the truth, Taris thought, but close enough.

'He certainly had good taste in books. I have looked over the shelves in his room and have decided that even the public reading rooms in London do not have the breadth of topic his library has.'

'A characteristic he inherited from our father.' Taris was careful in his choice of words and when his sister Lucy appeared at the doorway the family was quick to drop the subject altogether.

'Why did your brother leave Falder?' Bea asked the question again an hour later when she was alone with Taris.

'He killed my father.' The four words were enunciated without emotion.

'He shot him?'

'Nothing as dramatic as that. He just decided that the English system of privilege was not for him and left. All might have been more easily forgiven had our father not been in the throes of a severe winter ague. It was the opinion of the physician at the time that Cristo's disappearance killed him.'

'Disappearance?'

'He left no note. It was only later that one did come and by then our father was long dead. When we tried to locate Cristo he had no wish to be found and sent a message to that effect. As the years mounted we decided to respect his wishes.'

'But your mother…'

'Still loves him. He played the piano well and every so often she fancies she hears music coming from his room.' Bea noticed the way he turned from her as he told her, as though perhaps his mother was not the only one who missed a Falder son.

Bending to a drawer in a desk, he brought out a dark blue box and handed it to her. 'When I inherited my uncle's estates I also inherited his family jewels. They are kept here as I had no use for them. Is this something you might wish to wear?'

An intricate gold-and-topaz necklace lay in a white satin interior and to each side matching earrings were embedded.

'Oh, I could not accept such a thing.'

She was speechless and honoured. This was no insignificant piece. If she wore this, everyone would know where it had come from.

'There are many others should you want to sort through them as I cannot make out any of their forms.'

Carte blanche. Not a little offer. Still, she would rather have had the words that she had given him so many times last night.

I love you.

In this room with his hair pulled back into a queue he looked like a man who might never give her them back. Not in the daylight, with the voice of sanity and restraint between them and his lack of sight a potent reason for his reticence.

Darkness was their milieu, she decided, when the tendrils of night reduced any difference and the language between their bodies demanded no words.

Lord, even now the memory of it made her blush. As though he felt it too, his hand came against hers in a simple gesture, and the box of jewellery was laid down upon the desk, forgotten.

'Beatrice?' A question.

'Yes.' An answer.

The heavy slam of his heart was visible in the pulse at his throat. Not as unaffected as she might imagine.

She felt his hand skim across the line of her bottom and lift her skirt. The other one loosened his lacings and tilted her hips, entering slick wet and wanted, his breath against her throat as he pushed in further, no softness at all in it. Sheathed and tight. Full and intimate. Cold oak against the warmth of flesh, and the door unlocked.

Still, she could not pull back as his movements quickened, her hands splayed across the blotter, her head rolling as the same magic took her by surprise.

Anywhere? He could take her anywhere and she would follow? Her whimpers were quietened by his mouth as he covered the gathering waves of release and she was tipped into the place where nothing at all mattered.

He did not let her go when they had finished. Did not move apart or relinquish his tight grasp of her, his breath hoarse and the joining of their bodies tight in want.

'God.' Only that above the sound of breath, and the feel of cold air against her bare skin was sinful and exciting. The hot squeeze of his manhood still within her and the daylight exposing everything that night-time never had.

When his hands slid to where his body still lingered, she merely opened her legs further and let him explore, the scent of their lovemaking musky in the air around them.

'More,' she whispered and his answering laugh was as unguarded as she had ever heard it.

'Much more,' he returned as his fingers found a spot that made her whole body blush.

The sound of the clock brought them back and she had never felt so deliciously decadent as she ran her tongue across the outline of his lips.

'Taris?'

His eyes sharpened as her fingers traced the scar across his left eye, the trail beginning in his hairline and finishing on the rise of his cheekbone.

Had any lover ever touched him in the way she was doing now? By the way he stayed so very still she thought not.

'Did it hurt?'

The amber of his irises was brittle gold. 'At first it did, though the ocean saved me, I suspect, for the salt leached away the pain. By the time we reached land again I could barely feel it.'

'How long were you in the water?'

'So many hours that we lost count. With the blood loss from this it was Ashe who dragged me with him finally, though the currents did their part in the rescue and deposited us on land on our second evening afloat.'

'I have never heard any of this even whispered!' she said.

'Because of Emerald. It was her father who had caused the problem in the first place.'

'Her father?'

'Beau Sandford.'

'The pirate? I am beginning to think that your family has as many secrets as I do.'

'Which is why I tell them to you in the first place. Were you a woman without any past, I could not say a word.'

'I would always take care of any confidences, no matter what.'

He smiled. 'I know.'

* * *

Lord, Taris thought as he dressed that evening for the Davis country ball. He should tell Bea of his feelings for her, but something stopped him.

His blindness, if the truth were to be told and a dependence that he found repugnant, for the dream had been coming more frequently lately. The dream of the darkness without even a hint of light, lost in eternal black. The weariness and worry of it left him on edge but the child they had conceived together was also growing and the words that Beatrice had given him in the light of day as they made love demanded a response. From him.

Could he tell her everything?

Tell her of his fear and abhorrence of dependence and of pity. Tell her that his relationships with others were harder to maintain now with the sludge thicker, and negotiating a room full of people almost impossible without help.

Her help. He liked the feel of her arm against his, guiding him, lightly. He liked the way she stayed with him and talked, her easy conversation allowing him time to adjust and to avoid the pitfalls that he so often encountered.

He seldom took risks and yet today he had known that the door was unlocked. Anyone might have walked in. His fists tightened at his side as he realised what was happening to him.

Bea was making him live again. Live again even with the fear of tripping up, of being exposed, of having others seeing him in a compromised position.

He swallowed and swallowed again. If he lost her… No, he shook his head. He would not lose her, ever, and tonight when they were home from the party he swore that he would make her understand exactly what she meant to him and why.

Chapter Fifteen

Taris led Beatrice into the Davis soirée, his hand across her own.

'I seldom attended these sort of outings until recently,' he said to her as they came into the ballroom.

She smiled. 'What has changed your mind, my lord?'

'You by my side.' His eyes softened as he said it.

'A lovely compliment,' she returned.

'Oh, I have many more, Beatrice-Maude. Later tonight, if you would let me, I could share them with you.'

'Later tonight?' she queried with a laugh. 'Is that a promise?'

'Indeed.' The humour in his voice was easily heard. 'And may I say that you look very beautiful this evening.'

'You can see me?'

'Imagination has its advantages.'

'Such as?'

'In my mind you are wearing the gown drenched in perfume that I found you in after returning from London.'

'Rather revealing at a country ball?'

'And your hair is down, floating in curls around your shoulders like the sirens on the rocks at Li Galli.'

'If you heard me sing you might choose another analogy, my lord.'

'Boudicca, then, of the Iceni, leading the Ancient Britons against the Romans?'

'With poor Nero and his legions such an easy target!'

When they had both stopped laughing, she brought her fingers along the edge of his cheek.

'Taris?'

He was very still and in the amber of his eyes she determined a vulnerability that she had never seen there before.

'Yes?'

'Thank you.'

'For what?'

'For making me believe that I am nearly beautiful.'

'Ahh, Beatrice,' he returned and held her closer, 'to me you are very much more than that.'

An hour or so later Taris sensed that something was not right. He felt it in the air around him, and in the tension inside him.

Leaving Bea with Emerald and Ashe, he went with Bates on the pretence of retrieving his glasses from his cape.

Normally he would have simply sent his servant, but tonight the prickling sense of unease that he so often had had in his years as an intelligence officer under Wellington was strong, and he needed the silence to listen. As he sifted his way through the crowds, the intuition that had saved him on the Continent was heightened here and intense.

As they gained the entrance hall he heard a muffled thump followed by a distinct groan. Bates drew away, his footsteps easily heard on the marbled flooring, and then another noise followed the first.

'Bates?' When his servant did not answer, Taris released the diamond points of his ring before unshackling the handle of his cane.

'Bates?' He tried again, feeling a shadow on his skin and a bristling sense of danger. Reaching out, he tried to fend off whatever was coming at him and the glancing angle of a hard wooden object skimmed the flesh on his forearm in a heavy well-aimed blow; a baton if he should make a guess, but his initial twist had been enough to escape the worst of the jolt. The scent of bergamot was strong.

Radcliff! He was here? Raising his sword, Taris slashed before him, but all that was left was air.

Panic settled across calmness as he crouched to his servant on the floor at his feet. Another man lay beside him. Both were out cold, but still breathing.

God. Now the clerk would be after Bea!

Standing, he made for the noise in the room he had just left, running full into a door left half-open. On the rebound his fingers glanced across a pillar he had felt a few moments earlier and, gaining direction, he continued on, the feel of the wall against his palm and then the door. The warmth generated by a great amount of people led him onwards, and in the sludge of grey he determined shapes.

Someone swore at him as he bumped against a hand holding a glass, but he strode past, calling Beatrice's name as he went. Not softly either. Another person's foot almost tripped him up and he struggled to keep his balance, slamming into a plant that he had not seen and knocking it over.

No longer careful or camouflaged.

Years of restraint were lost in that one single moment of imagining her being hurt and as people came within his sphere he made no attempt at apology, their loud exclamations ignored completely as he made his way further inside.

'Beatrice?' Nothing else mattered now save finding out where she was, though without Bates at his side Taris had little idea of where that might be or of the objects in his way. A chair stopped his progress and he turned to the left.

'Beatrice-Maude?' His voice was louder, the cadence hardly recognisable, and the band that had been playing at this end of the room wound down into silence as he continued to shout. His breath came in thick bands of fear and he widened his eyes in an attempt to see something more.

Ghosts of grey blurred into blackness, ephemeral and unrecognisable, the darker shadows of walls giving him at least a clue of the boundaries in the room. Beyond that, bands of sombre murkiness lingered, the detail of the chamber completely lost.

'Beatrice? Where are you?' His unsheathed silver blade caused those around him to scatter.

'Wellingham has a sword. He's gone bloody mad.'

The sound of screaming made the hair on his arms stand up and the back of his neck crawl.

'Bea?' Had Radcliff got to her? Was he pulling her outside even as he searched hopelessly through the haze?

One man tried to stop him, but Taris made short work of the fellow, the fop's ineffective jab no match at all for a soldier trained in the art of warfare for over six years. He felt others move back from him, whispering, the footfalls of people afraid.

'Taris?' Ashe's voice from afar, the sound in it almost as desperate as his own. Relief surged through him.

'Asher, can you see Beatrice?' The room seemed larger than it had all night, and still there was no response from the only one he sought.

'Bea. Beatrice-Maude, where are you? If you touch her, Radcliff, I will kill you. I swear I will. Ashe?' Another shout to his brother, who sounded closer.

'The clerk is here?' Asher's tone sounded exactly like his own, and the noise of those in the room lessened, as though they too were suddenly cognisant of further threat and waiting for it to charge at them from any quarter.

'Beatrice?' He tried to disguise panic, but couldn't.

'To your right. We are over here, Taris.' His sister-in-law's voice and then finally Beatrice.

'Taris?' Her question was filled with worry. Closer and closer. The whirl of blackness made him pant, the sweat on his brow building and then she was there beside him, her hands threaded around his arm and the smell of violets welcome.

'I thought I had lost you. Radcliff is here.' He gathered her in, sword at ready. If anyone came close he would kill them, he swore that he would. The grey sludge of nothingness clung to his fear and anger made him shake. Only they in the room against the world!

'Taris. He is not here. I cannot see him here.' Beatrice's reason was calming.

'You are sure?'

'He is not here.'

The roar of the crowd came back and the thrump of his blood beating in his temples lessened. When Ashe and Emerald joined them, he lowered his blade and tried to find a normal breath.

'He's gone. The bastard was here, but now he has gone.'

'You are sure it was Radcliff?'

'I could smell him.'

'Are you drunk, Wellingham?' Lord Davis's voice beside him voiced the query.

'Not…drunk.' He could barely get the words out, the rush of relief making him feel light-headed. 'I believe that there is a man here who might hurt Mrs Bassingstoke and I would protect her. He has already knocked out two men.'

A hum of conversation erupted.

'Describe him for them, Bea,' he ordered and was pleased when she began to talk, giving him a moment to try to collect himself.

Beatrice felt his heart beating hard against her back. His arms had not released her and she stood in the middle of a roomful of strangers all looking at her.

Well, at Taris, were the truth to be told, because he appeared so dangerously and wildly magnificent with the scar across his eye and the sword in his hand, threatening anyone who made the mistake of placing themselves between them. Even Ashe stood his distance and waited. For reason!

'He is a very tall and thin man with light brown hair and a small moustache.'

She peered around as the others did, but Radcliff was nowhere in sight, either in this room or in the next one.

'I am sure he has left,' she said more quietly to Taris and because of it he released her. Still, he held her hand as though he would not let her out of his sight.

She smiled at her choice of words. Out of his touch, more like, the whole evening taking on an importance that almost brought her to her knees.

For a man who hated to draw attention to himself tonight had been a revelation. Taris Wellingham had not only shouted across the room for all to hear, but had shielded her with his own body when he perceived the threat as ominous.

A declaration?

Perhaps he had not said he cared for her yet, but actions spoke louder than any words. Her fingers curled into his and stayed there. Safe. Right. Dependable.

Asher and Emerald next to her completed the guard.

A family who would stand at her side as no others ever had before.

When Bates came up to join them, the bump on his forehead was raw and bleeding.

'Did you see who hit you?' Taris asked as he realised his man was standing beside him.

'I just saw the baton. Presumably the same weapon he used on the footman, who is now being tended to by the housekeeper. It was a constable's baton.'

'The policeman who helped me off the street said he had lost his baton that day.' Beatrice wished she might have kept that piece of information to herself as Taris swore soundly.

She noticed Bates had given him back the cane's wooden cover and saw how well the sword was sheathed within it, the silver ball forming part of the hilt of the weapon.

To each side of them a line of people had formed, the interest on their faces undisguised.

Taris, however, seemed unaware of any of it as he took Bea's fingers and placed them in the crook of his arm.

'We will follow you out, Bates,' he said and the small party walked as one to the waiting conveyance.

At Falder they sat in the small blue salon and tried to make sense of what had just happened.

'The man must be crazy to think to attack us there.' Ashe had a glass of wine in his hand. Emerald sat beside him with an identical glass.

'I am not sure he meant to,' Taris interjected. 'I think we surprised him. If I were to guess I would imagine he was waiting for when we left to attack. But when he saw there were only two of us and that in the darkness he had surprise as an advantage, he took his opportunity.'

'Bates will have a damn headache in the morning. You were lucky he didn't go for you, Taris.'

'He did.' Rolling back his sleeve, Beatrice saw a large discoloured lump on his forearm, the skin broken by the force of the blow. 'I felt him there—' He stopped, tilting his head as though trying to remember something else.

'Not all bergamot,' he said suddenly. 'Hops and mead. The smell of hops and mead.'

'The Dog and the Boar?' Ashe was on his feet.

'At Kenworth.'

Taris turned with his brother and before Beatrice had a chance to say goodbye they were gone, calling men to join them.

Emerald had not moved, though she took a large swallow of her wine before beginning to speak.

'The Dog and the Boar is a tavern five miles from here which has rooms for travellers. It makes its own special type of mead.'

'The one that Taris could smell?'

'Exactly. If Radcliff is there he doesn't stand a chance.'

'They would kill him?' Horror made her whisper.

Emerald laughed. 'Worse. When they finish with him he might wish that he were dead.'

'He could be waiting for them!' The danger of it all made her voice shake. 'He could have others with him!'

'I think our men can hold their own.' Emerald's reply held no sense of any fear.

'Are you always so certain?'

Emerald began to laugh. 'You think that of me when I could say exactly the same of you.'

'The same?' Bea frowned.

'Your discussions! You manage your salon with the acumen of one long used to people and the subjects you put forward are not for the fainthearted. And yet you allow all an opinion, no matter how unusual.'

'I was not allowed my own for so many years that I suspect it is now a calling to hear those of others.'

'Are you never fearful that such debate might get out of hand?'

'It is London. What harm could my patrons truly do?'

'Crucify you with words, for one.'

'The opinions of those here at Falder are the only ones I worry about.'

'Lord. No wonder Taris wants you by his side, Bea. Together you might rule the world. I hope that he doesn't take you off to Beaconsmeade too quickly.'

The conversation whirled again out of kilter. 'I don't understand.'

'Tonight was the first time that he has ever forgotten to hide his lack of sight from others and that was because of his fear for your safety.'

'Or perhaps for that of our child.' Bea had not meant to say it but it slipped out. Unbidden.

'Which explains your penchant for weak tea?'

'Anything else makes me feel ill.'

'Have you wondered why a man who is pursued by every eligible miss in London has no other offspring, given that he is now almost thirty-two years of age?'

'Perhaps he has been careful?'

'Or celibate. Before you he barely noticed women and when he inherited his estate, believe me, there were many vying for his attention. You sell yourself short by proclaiming that his interest lies only in this child, for I can see that you love him.'

A single tear traced its way down Beatrice's cheek. 'I do,' she returned, no longer able to hide anything. 'More than life itself, for he has saved me by letting me be me.'

'Then when he returns tell him how you feel, but be warned. The Wellingham men are not prone to using much poetry in words, so listen for them in other ways.'

'Other ways?'

His arms around her at the ball encircling her in his safety and protecting her from an enemy he could not even see. His breath hoarse as he called to her, no touchstone for his hands and his man Bates nowhere in sight.

Other ways? How many had she seen tonight? Bravery had a face as did panic, written into fear and honour as he went about the daunting task of finding her in a crowded room and risking everything.

And exposing everything!

She had heard the whispers as they left.

'Can he see anything?'

'My God, is Wellingham blind?'

Taris would have heard the conjecture too, but he had not made any mention of it, his careful masking of poor sight for years banished in those moments of terror.

For her! Everything he had held so close abandoned because of his fear for her.

Bea's heart ached with the sheer breadth and depth of his gift.

Taris and Asher returned almost two hours later with the story of Radcliff's capture. The clerk had been surprised by their arrival and had instantly surrendered, his lack of any resistance making the task of apprehending him relatively speedy. After leaving him safely in the hands of the local constabulary there was no more to be done.

'James Radcliff confessed to everything from the taking of the Bassingstoke money to paying someone to keep you out of the way, Beatrice, whilst he searched the confines of your home.' Taris sat next to her and had taken her hand in his as he related the story. 'He also said that his intentions were never to kill you, though given the lengths he went to retrieve the ledgers I find that hard to believe.'

'It was all about getting back the books?'

'With them destroyed Radcliff believed he could walk free. He thought they were with you in the carriage and was following behind you until the snowstorm forced him to take refuge at a tavern. He then believed you had taken them to London.'

'But I didn't.'

'Robert Nelson said they had been sent to you after the death of your husband. At a guess I would say they were packed up with the rest of your belongings and now lie beneath the snow in the spot where the carriage rolled after Radcliff tampered with the axle.'

'But why would he take the money in the first place? Surely he realised the amounts would be written and recorded?'

'Grandeur, I think. Nelson alluded to the fact he was the second son of a mayor somewhere to the north. A son who thought he was entitled to more.'

'So the amount stolen is in the books?'

Taris nodded. 'These things have a way of coming out, no matter how carefully they are managed. He will stand trial for tampering with a public conveyance and for the embezzlement of funds that did not belong to him. Gaol will be his home for a good many years, and I will follow his progress to make certain that he never comes near us again.'

'The man must have been mad to think he could come to take you from us.' Emerald stood beside her, the tone in her voice leaving no doubt as to what she thought of Radcliff's motives.

Asher laughed. 'We cannot keep Beatrice here, Em. She belongs to my brother.'

'Yes, she does.' Taris's voice was firm and for the very first time in her whole life Beatrice knew the true meaning of place.

* * *

An hour later Bea lay tucked up beside Taris, the light of only a small slice of moon making her think again of Maldon and the snowstorm.

How far had they come? How far were they yet to go? A soft flutter in her stomach made her take in air and gasp.

'I felt it. I felt our baby move. Like a butterfly.' She took his hand and laid it across her stomach, staying very still and when the child jumped again he pulled back in surprise and delight. No sight needed. Just touch and feel. A first for them both. Entire, complete and elemental. The beginning of a journey that would take them places neither had even dreamed of.

'If I had lost you tonight…' Taris could not finish and swallowed heavily before beginning again. 'If I lost you, I don't think that I could live.'

Tears welled in her eyes.

'Others may now know of your secret. I heard people talking as we left the Davis function…'

He stopped the words by laying a finger upon her lips. 'I love you, Beatrice-Maude Bassingstoke.'

His voice was rusty, as if the words were ones he had not thought to say. 'I love you so damn much that it hurts.' His hand fell across his heart, opened like a fan. 'Here.'

She saw him take in a breath, finding time and fighting an emotion that was too new and too foreign, secrets and privacy overwhelmed by the honest confession of love. His love for her!

Laying her palm across his, she held on to the warmth and brought his fingers to her lips, kissing each one by one by one, smiling as he turned towards her.

Then she forgot to think at all.

Epilogue

Doctor MacLaren delivered two healthy sons in September, the second baby arriving twelve minutes after the first.

When the ministrations of the birth were finally completed and they had a moment alone together, Beatrice watched her husband run his fingers across them, gently, as they lay in the bassinet by her bed. She watched how he checked the number of fingers and toes and the fragile lines of their bodies. Still, there were things that he could not know by touch and she tried to give them to him.

'Their hair is black like yours, Taris, and the colour of their eyes is…undecipherable.'

He laughed and the gold ring she had placed on his marriage finger four months earlier glinted.

'They are very small and very perfect. Almost as perfect as my wife,' he added and looked up.

In the light you could see the opaqueness in his eyes had worsened and Bea knew that the darkness he had always feared would soon come.

Yet it did not matter! Surrounded by love and released from pretence, her husband had finally accepted the fact that the worth of a man was not something measured simply by his ability to see.

No, it was measured in love and strength and honour and decency.

And family, she added as the door to their bedroom opened and the rest of the Wellingham family streamed in.

HISTORICAL

Novels coming in February 2010

THE RAKE AND THE HEIRESS
Marguerite Kaye

Any virtuous society lady knows to run from Mr Nicholas Lytton.
But he's the one person who can unlock the mystery surrounding
Lady Serena Stamppe's inheritance. Accepting Nicholas's offer
of assistance, Serena soon discovers the forbidden thrills
of liaising with a libertine – excitement, scandal…and a most
pleasurable seduction!

WICKED CAPTAIN, WAYWARD WIFE
Sarah Mallory

When young widow Evelina Wylder comes face to face
with her dashing captain husband – *very* much alive – she's
shocked, overjoyed…and so furious she's keeping Nick firmly
out of their marriage bed! Now the daring war hero faces
his biggest challenge – proving to Eve that his first duty is
to love and cherish her, forever!

THE PIRATE'S WILLING CAPTIVE
Anne Herries

Instinct told her that Captain Justin Sylvester was a man
she could trust. Captive on the high seas, with nowhere to run,
curiously Maribel Sanchez had never felt more free. Now she had
to choose: return to rigid society and become an old man's
unwilling wife or stay as Justin's more than *willing* mistress…

MILLS & BOON

HISTORICAL

**Another exciting novel available
this month:**

THE CAPTAIN'S MYSTERIOUS LADY

Mary Nichols

She's revived his heart – but who is she?

Driven by grief and an implacable thirst for vengeance, Captain James Drymore has one sole purpose in life: to hunt down the men who killed his wife. But when he sees a beautiful young lady in distress James allows himself to become distracted for the first time…

Having rescued Amy, James discovers she didn't escape unscathed – she has lost her memory! As the conflicted Captain slowly puts together the complex pieces of his mysterious lady's past, James realises he needs to let go of his own. Can he and Amy build a new future – together?

**The Piccadilly Gentlemen's Club
Seeking justice, finding love**

MILLS & BOON®

HISTORICAL

Another exciting novel available this month:

THE MAJOR AND THE PICKPOCKET

Lucy Ashford

"Trying to escape, were you?"

Tassie bit her lip. Why hadn't he turned her over to the constables? She certainly wasn't going to try to run past him, even if he did have a limp. She was tall, but this man towered over her – six foot of hardened muscle, shoulders forbiddingly broad beneath his riding coat, strong booted legs set firmly apart. Major Marcus Forrester. All ready for action.

And Tassie couldn't help but remember his kiss…

MILLS & BOON®